WILD JUSTICE

TYSON WILD BOOK TWO

TRIPP ELLIS

WELCOME

Want more books like this?

You'll probably never hear about my new releases unless you join my newsletter.

SIGN UP HERE

1

———

"**I** need you to get down here, ASAP," a gruff voice said, crackling through the tiny speaker in my cell phone.

I had barely managed to find the phone and answer it before it stopped ringing. Not many people have this number, so I figured it was worth answering. My eyes weren't even open yet, and it took me a moment to process what I was hearing. I was having one of those crazy dreams that didn't make any sense. In the dream, I was a Formula One race car driver, and I had just gotten a $100 million dollar contract from Ferrari. But we weren't racing on a track. We were speeding through the desert. Needless to say, the car was having trouble trying to get over the sand dunes. Like I said, it made no sense. It made coming back to reality that much harder.

"Sheriff?" my voice scratched out.

"When do you think you can be here?"

"Where is here?" I asked, wiping the sleep from my eyes, trying to force them awake.

"Pearl Beach."

"Yeah," I grumbled. "Give me 20 minutes."

"Make it 10!"

He hung up the phone before I could ask him what this was about.

It was pitch dark in my stateroom.

My eyes squinted as I looked at the display on my phone, not yet used to the brightness. After a moment, I was able to focus.

4:22 AM.

What the hell did Sheriff Wayne Daniels want at 4:22 AM?

I delicately grabbed the sultry brunette's arm that was wrapped around me and moved it aside. Aria was out like a rock. We had just gone to sleep a few hours earlier, and she wasn't much of a morning person, anyway.

I pulled the covers aside and slid out of bed, trying not to wake her. I hated to leave her. She lay like an angel, her pert ass beckoning a second glance. I knew I was going to miss out on our morning ritual together, which I had grown quite accustomed to.

I fumbled for my boxers that I wore the night before. They were in a ball on the deck next to Aria's panties. I pulled them on and followed the trail of clothes, like breadcrumbs, that led into the salon. We had started pulling each other's clothes off the minute we entered the hatch. We'd been together for a few weeks now, and I couldn't get enough.

I pulled on a pair of shorts and a T-shirt, slipped on some

shoes, and grabbed my Köenig-Haas MMX 9mm. I press-checked the weapon and slipped the holster inside my waistband for an appendix carry. Then I grabbed a Diet Coke from the fridge and pushed through the hatch into the cockpit.

Fresh air filled my lungs as I breathed deep and stretched. The marina was quiet, and gentle waves lapped against the hull of the boat. It was calm and peaceful.

I was still living on JD's 45 foot sport fishing boat. The rent was free as long as I helped him out with charters here and there. It was a sweet gig, and I didn't plan on changing my residence anytime soon.

I headed down the dock toward *Diver Down*, and had an Uber pick me up in the parking lot.

I figured if I was in some kind of trouble, Sheriff Daniels would have showed up and arrested me, personally. Maybe he was too lazy and wanted me to come to him?

It took five minutes for the Uber to show up, and another five to get over to Pearl Beach. Coconut Key was a small island, and at this time of the morning there was no traffic. *Not like there was much traffic during rush hour, anyway.*

I arrived on the scene 16 minutes after I spoke with the sheriff, and that seemed to be good enough for him. He had bigger fish to fry.

The area was sectioned off with yellow police tape, and the medical examiner poked at the body. Forensics investigators snapped photographs, brilliant flashes reflecting against the water.

The sand shifted under my feet as I marched toward the

crime scene. The gentle crashing waves on the beach were soothing, in stark contrast to the corpse that lay against the white sand.

Gulls picked at its pale flesh. Crabs and other scavengers tried to abscond with tiny morsels. It was a gruesome sight that made me cringe.

But I had seen plenty of dead bodies in my day.

There were a few chunks of flesh missing where a shark had taken a nibble. But that's not what caused this man's death. You don't go swimming in slacks and a dress shirt. Of course, he could have fallen overboard from a yacht, but something told me there were more sinister forces at play.

"I didn't do it, I swear," I said, raising my hands innocently.

Sheriff Daniels scowled at me. Perhaps it was too early for my demented sense of humor?

2

J D strolled down the beach like he owned the place. His long blonde hair flowed with the breeze. Or should I say, mostly gray hair? He wore his usual attire—cargo shorts, Hawaiian shirt, and a pair of dark sunglasses—even though it was pitch black outside. He looked like an aging rock star, and he was quite proud of the fact.

Sheriff Daniels must have called him as well. Why the hell did he want us here?

Jack Donovan took his time walking down the beach. When he arrived at the scene, he said, "I see he recruited you too?"

"Yeah, but I'm not sure why?" I said.

"Who's the floater?" JD asked, nodding to the body.

Sheriff Daniels' eyes narrowed at Jack. "Have a little more respect for the dead, JD. After all, it is one of your friends."

JD arched a concerned brow and pulled down his sunglasses to get a better look at the corpse.

We stood about 15 feet away from the body. The medical examiner, Brenda Sparks, hovered over the remains. She scowled at JD when she saw him and looked away, abruptly.

"Whoops," I said, knowing the two had hooked up before. At least, I assumed they did.

Brenda was cute-ish... If you'd been stranded on a desert island for a year.

"Trouble in paradise?" I asked.

JD glared at me. "Sometimes you gotta do what you gotta do. I jumped on the grenade so—" he stopped mid-sentence, realizing he probably shouldn't say out loud that he slept with her just to get information about our last case.

Sheriff Daniels shook his head. "I can't believe I'm going to do this."

"Do what?" I asked.

"That's Scott Kingston."

JD's face dropped. "Ah, shit!"

My face twisted, perplexed, not recognizing the name.

"Local boat dealer," Daniels said. "He's known for high-end yachts and go-fast boats, upscale sport-fishing boats. Pretty elite clientele. Along with some real scumbags. Sold JD his boat, if I'm not mistaken," the sheriff said, making a subtle jab.

"Our transaction was aboveboard," JD protested.

"I didn't say it wasn't," Daniels replied.

The two exchanged a suspicious glance.

"That's a damn shame," JD said. "He threw some great parties. There was this one time..."

"Not now, JD," the Sheriff barked

"What have you got so far?" I asked.

"Looks like a professional hit. Two to the back of the head. Small caliber. Brenda is trying to ascertain the time of death."

"He's been in the water for a while," JD said, surveying the remains.

"Who found the body?" I asked.

"Couple of tourists. They came down to the beach for a little romp when Scott put a damper on things."

"Did you talk to them already?" I asked.

"I took their statements. They're from Iowa. It's pretty clear they didn't have anything to do with this. She's a school-teacher, and he works in construction."

JD and I exchanged a curious glance.

"So, why are we here?" I asked.

The sheriff let out a distressed sigh. "Like I said, I'm going to regret this." He cleared his throat. "Deputy Perkins resigned. He's going back to Oklahoma. That leaves me short-staffed. Considering your backgrounds, and your help on the last case—and since I know you two can't keep your noses out of anything—I'm deputizing you both."

JD's eyes brightened, and a grin tugged on his lips.

"I don't know about this," I said.

"What's not to know?" JD asked. "We'll have a badge and a gun and we can shoot people!"

The sheriff rolled his eyes. "You can't shoot people."

"Hell, I can shoot people with or without your badge," JD said. "I've been doing it my whole life."

"I can change my mind at any time," the sheriff said

"No need. We'll make great deputies," JD said. His eyes flicked to mine. "Won't we?"

"I appreciate the gesture, Sheriff. But honestly, I came down here to get away from all this."

"I'm sorry to hear that, because I think you would be a huge asset to the department." He pleaded his case. "I'm just a small-town cop in over his head. I'm trying to keep this whole thing together, without enough money and too little resources. The last thing I need are tourists finding dead bodies washed up on shore. And that's starting to become a regular thing." He paused for a moment, then he swung for the fence. "And, I figured with your personal background, what with your parents and all, you'd be all over this."

He *had* to pull out my parents. He knew there was no way I could turn this down.

"You'd have access to all the department's resources, including the files regarding your parents' murders," he said, putting a cherry on top.

"Okay. Fine," I said. "I'll help out."

"It's just temporary," Daniels said. He dug into his pocket and handed us both shiny gold badges that said *Coconut County Sheriff's Deputy* on them.

"Who was the last person to see Scott Kingston alive?"

Sheriff Daniels shrugged. "That's what I just hired you boys to find out."

3

"Special Agent Archer, FBI," a woman said as she approached the crime scene.

She flashed a badge, then slipped it back into her pocket. She looked like a typical Fed—navy blazer, white blouse, navy slacks, aviator sunglasses.

It didn't take much investigating to see that she had some hidden talent underneath that pantsuit. JD nudged an elbow into my ribs, letting me know that he had discovered the same thing.

She was hot as hell.

Wavy, sandy-blonde hair, blue eyes, sculpted cheekbones, and pouty lips that could start wars.

Sheriff Daniels adjusted his duty belt, defensively. A beautiful woman was always welcome, but no local law enforcement liked the Feds stepping on their toes.

Agent Archer picked up on his posture. "Don't worry, I'm

not looking to interfere. I'd just like to share information. We had Kingston under surveillance."

"Obviously the surveillance was not that close," I said, dryly.

Her blue eyes threw daggers. "We can't be everywhere all the time."

"What was he under surveillance for?" Sheriff Daniels asked.

"I'm sorry, I can't divulge that information."

"I'm not exactly sure how you expect to exchange information if you aren't willing to share," Daniels said.

"The investigation is ongoing," Archer said. "Divulging any specifics may compromise our agents in the field."

Wayne forced a smile. In the most insincere tone he could muster, he said, "Well, since you put it that way. I'll be sure to let you know the minute we have any information."

She dug into her pocket and handed him a card. "Thanks. I appreciate your cooperation."

Archer whirled around and sauntered away. JD and I couldn't help but fixate on her luscious assets.

"Now why did you have to go run her off?" JD said, half joking.

Sheriff Daniels frowned at JD. "I'm not running a dating service here. Don't you two have a murder to solve?"

"Since we're officially *on the job*, does that mean we have an expense account?" JD asked

"I don't even have an expense account. I'm regretting this already. Now get out of here before I change my mind."

"Come on," I said. Let's go grab some breakfast. Discuss the case."

I followed JD to his red Porsche parked in one of the public lots near the beach. I climbed into the passenger side of the convertible Carrera, and JD brought the engine to life with a roar. He dropped it into gear, and the tires spit gravel as we peeled out of the parking lot.

Wind rustled through my hair, and the flat six screamed as the sun crested the horizon. JD kept the stereo at an earsplitting level, pounding my eardrums with hits from the 80s.

JD had two speeds. Fast, and faster.

The bucket seat hugged my form as we twisted around corners, testing the limits of the car's grip on the road. A few moments later, we pulled into the parking lot of Wilford's Waffle House. A cute little hostess escorted us to a booth, and we slid into the green vinyl seats.

The place was already full with seniors looking to catch the morning special. It had an old-school diner vibe. Checkered tile floor. Jukebox. It served breakfast 24 hours a day. It was popular with the late night drunk crowd.

"Your waitress will be with you in a few minutes," the hostess said as she handed us laminated menus.

I had been here many times before, and had my eye on a fat stack of blueberry pancakes, slathered with butter and maple syrup.

When the waitress arrived, JD ordered a ham and cheese

omelette and some crispy bacon. The waitress poured us some coffee and sent our ticket back to the cook.

The light murmur of chatter filled the air along with the clink of forks against plates. I usually didn't get out much for breakfast. I'd roll out of bed and whip something together in the galley of the *Slick'n Salty*.

"How well did you know Kingston?" I asked.

JD shrugged. "I bought the boat from him. He threw regular parties and invited his clients. The guy was always surrounded by hotties. He certainly worked hard at customer retention. Once he sold you a boat, you were in his extended family, so to speak. He didn't ever want you to buy another boat anywhere else. He could get anything you needed at decent prices. He was the go to guy. Celebrities, drug dealers, tech giants—didn't matter. They'd all mingle together at his parties like it was no big deal."

"Can you think of anybody who would want him dead?"

"I think we should probably start with the basics. Talk to his girlfriend. See if there's anybody he owed money to."

"Maybe one of his clients got pissed off? Found a better deal somewhere else?"

"The kind of people Kingston dealt with weren't really price sensitive. These are cats with money to burn."

I looked up from the menu and saw Special Agent Archer lingering at the hostess stand. She surveyed the restaurant, like any good field agent would, and her eyes met mine.

I tried not to frown and muttered, "Look who just showed up."

JD craned his neck over his shoulder. "Well, would you look at that?"

Archer whispered something to the hostess, and a fraction of a second later they were both headed in our direction.

"You boys don't mind if I join you, do you?" Archer said as she slipped into the booth beside JD. The hostess left another laminated menu and sauntered back to her stand.

"Go right ahead," I said.

She smiled. "We didn't really get to meet on the beach. "Jen Archer," she said, extending her hand across the table.

I shook her delicate hand. "Tyson Wild."

Her hand was soft, and she had a nice manicure. She didn't wear any rings, on either hand.

"This is Jack Donovan," I added.

"Pleasure to meet you both. And your involvement in the case is...?"

"Deputy Sheriff," JD said with a boastful tone. He was enjoying the badge way too much.

I wanted to roll my eyes.

"And how long have you been working with the sheriff?"

I looked at my watch. "Oh, about 30 minutes now."

Her eyes narrowed at me. "Sheriff must have a great deal of faith in you."

I smiled. "Let's just say I have a certain set of skills."

"Really? What's your background?"

"What's *your* background?" I asked with a slightly sassy tone.

"I asked you first." She grinned.

"What you'll be able to find out about me will largely depend on your security clearance. Even then, you'll probably come up with nothing."

"One of those, are you?"

"Could be." I had no doubt that she was going to run my background. It would only leave her with more questions.

She turned her attention to JD. "What about you? Karaoke DJ?"

JD smiled. "Not me. I'm retired. Former Spec-War Operator. Did a little time with the company. Now I live a life of leisure."

"Let me guess," Archer mused. "You two knew each other in the service. Ran a few ops together. You look like you may have been a company man." Her eyes narrowed. "But, then you stepped out on your own for more lucrative offers. Am I close?"

"You do have a fascinating imagination," I said.

She smiled a cocksure grin, knowing she was right. She was good. I had to give her that.

"So, I've got a couple of real cowboys here."

"I always preferred the term *outlaw* myself," JD said.

Archer's smile faded. "Let's get one thing straight. I don't know why Sheriff Daniels deputized you, and I don't care. But you better play this one by the rules. If you run across anything that you think I might need to know about, you tell me. I have an active investigation going on, and the last thing I need is you two *outlaws* fucking this up. Lives are at stake. Are we clear?"

"Now, sugar, we wouldn't dream of screwing up your little investigation," JD said.

"I'd like a heads up before you make any moves. Just a professional courtesy."

"I'll see what we can do," I said.

Our waitress returned with our breakfast. She clanked the plates across the table. "Ma'am, would you like to order?"

"No, thank you. I was just leaving." Archer slid out of the booth.

"Can I get you gentlemen anything else?" the waitress asked.

4

"She's a little spitfire, isn't she?" JD said.

"I get the impression she didn't like us very much," I replied.

"What's not to like?" He shoveled in another mouthful.

"I'm sure she could come up with a list."

My phone buzzed in my pocket. I pulled it out and looked at the caller ID. Sheriff Daniels. I took the call, and the sheriff's voice crackled through the speaker. He didn't bother to say *hello*. Just stated the facts. "The ME puts time of death around three weeks ago, give or take. Some kind of larva growing in the corpse. I don't know how that stuff works. His girlfriend filed a missing persons report a week and a half ago. Claire Hopkins. Why don't you guys go talk to her, see where it leads?"

"Right on it."

I hung up the phone and relayed the information to JD. I

looked at my watch. "Finish that up and run me by the boat. Maybe I can catch Aria just as she's waking up."

JD shook his head. "What is with you two?"

I shrugged.

"What am I supposed to do? Wait in the car while you get in a little quickie?"

"Basically."

"How about we take care of our business first?"

"I'll be able to think much clearer this way," I assured.

"This is starting to sound serious. I think you need counseling."

"What? She's hot. Young. Easy to be around. No drama."

JD scoffed.

"Don't hate."

"Have you registered yet? Should I buy you a toaster oven?"

"Fuuuck you," I said, playfully.

"I should start charging you for double occupancy on the boat."

"Just because you haven't found the next ex-Mrs. Donovan yet doesn't mean you have to spoil it for the rest of us."

"Oh, no. This is far more problematic than I thought. You think this woman could eventually be your ex-wife?"

I crinkled my brow at him. "No. I didn't say anything like that."

"But you're thinking it. Somewhere in the back of that twisted little head of yours, you're thinking she could be the one."

I rolled my eyes. "I'm not talking about this anymore."

There was a moment of silence before I had to defend myself.

"Look. I like her. What's the big deal?"

"That's how it starts. Like is a gateway word. Pretty soon you'll be using the other L word. And before you know it, you'll be depressed, alone, and she'll take half of everything you own."

"I don't own anything so, technically, that won't be a problem."

JD sighed. "You're farther gone than I thought. This is going to require an intervention."

"An intervention?" I asked with an arched eyebrow.

"Yes. Before it's too late."

JD shoveled the last bits of his omelette in his mouth, and I threw a wad of cash on the table to cover the tab and a healthy tip. I still had fat stacks of cash left over from my poker winnings.

"Let's go talk to this Claire Hopkins, then I'll swing you by the boat. I've got a meeting noon, so I'm on a little bit of a timetable."

I sighed. "Fine."

We left the diner and strolled through the parking lot. The air had the heavy smell of rain. Gray clouds gathered overhead. I climbed into JD's car and held on for dear life as we raced to Scott Kingston's home.

Claire Hopkins was living there. It was a luxurious place right on the beach. It had a mid-century modern feel to it with sleek, minimalist architecture and appointments. Claire pulled open the door after a few knocks, wearing a string bikini that struggled to contain pert assets. She had blonde hair, blue eyes, and tan skin. She looked like she belonged in the swimsuit edition of Sports Illustrated.

JD flashed his gold badge. He puffed out his chest and said, "Deputy Sheriff. Mind if we ask you a few questions."

A worried look washed over her face. "Is this about Scott?"

"I'm afraid so," I said.

She broke down in tears when we told her what happened. Her response seemed to be genuine. She invited us in, and we took a seat on the couch in the living room. From where I sat, I could see the beach, and the crashing waves of the ocean.

It was a nice place. No doubt about it.

Scott Kingston had done very well for himself in the boating business. The house was open and full of light. There were several pieces of art on the walls that had to set him back at least seven figures.

Once initial shock wore off, Claire was open to a few questions.

"You waited nearly a week and a half to report this? Why so long?" I asked.

"Scott was always disappearing for a few days here and

there. It wasn't unusual. Sometimes he'd take a boat up to Fort Lauderdale for a client, stay a few days, pick up another one and bring it back. I started to get really worried after week, then finally made the call."

"How long have you two been together?" I asked.

"A little over a year. But, *together* is kind of a loose term."

"What do you mean?" JD asked.

"I mean, let's be honest. Scott wasn't exactly a one-woman kind of guy."

"So, he was having an affair?" JD asked.

She laughed. "Please. Scott couldn't keep it in his pants."

"And that didn't bother you?" I asked.

"I'm not one of those girls who thinks they can actually change their man into something he's not. I liked Scott. We had fun together. And, he kept me in the lifestyle that I'm accustomed to. Besides, I had my own fun from time to time."

"And he was okay with that?" I asked.

"I didn't feel the need to broadcast it to him. We had an understanding." She hesitated. "We just didn't talk about it that much."

"Can you think of anyone who may have wanted him dead?" I continued.

"Where do you want me to start?"

5

"Scott was acting funny lately," Claire said. "He was nervous about something. But he wouldn't tell me what."

My phone buzzed again. This time it was Isabella. I didn't have time to take the call. She was my former handler at Cobra Company—a clandestine agency that did contract work for the CIA, and other three letter agencies. More often than not, when Isabella called it was not good. That was a life I was trying to put behind me.

"If you had to guess?" JD said.

"I know Scott was worried about Carlos. He just got released from prison. Did a nickel in Raiford."

"Why was he worried about Carlos?" I asked.

"He totally screwed the guy over! When Carlos got popped, Scott repossessed his boat. I don't know the ins and outs of the transaction, I just know that Carlos got the short end of the stick. Drug dealers don't like to keep assets in their name. Scott *leases* them the boat, so it can't be confiscated by the authorities when they're arrested. Sometimes Scott had to jump through hoops to protest the confiscation, but most of the time he came out on top."

Federal and local governments had been stealing property for years under the civil forfeiture laws. If a piece of property was used in the commission of a crime, it was fair game. Drinking and driving? Some municipalities would take your car. Pick up a hooker in a back alley? Some municipalities would take your car. Especially if they thought you didn't have the money to fight it. Until 2000, even if the owner had no knowledge of the criminal activity, the authorities could take the property and there was little or no recourse. The Supreme Court even upheld the decision. But in 2000, Congress passed the Civil Asset Forfeiture Reform Act— owners who did not consent to the illegal activity, nor had any knowledge of it, were protected.

It was debatable whether Scott knew the illegal activity of his clients, but with him as the *owner* of the property, he was usually able to avoid forfeiture.

"So you think Carlos may have killed him?" I asked.

"I don't know. Like I said. I don't know how his business really worked. Or who he owed money to."

"Do you know Carlos's last name?"

She thought for a moment. "No. Sorry." She paused. "There was another guy. Got into it with him at a party last month. Scott fucked his girlfriend. The guy wasn't too happy about that. He threatened to kill Scott. There were a bunch of witnesses. I figured it was all drunk bravado. But maybe not."

"Who was the guy?" I asked.

"Travis Wilkes." She nearly gagged as she said the words. "I hate that guy."

"You know where we can find him?" I asked.

"He lives on the island. You're cops. You can probably figure it out." She slumped. "So, we weren't married or anything. What's going to happen to me? Am I gonna get kicked out of this house?" Her worried eyes flicked between JD and me.

"That's probably a question for your attorney," JD said.

"I don't have one."

"You might want to get one," I said. "It depends if Scott had a will, and if you were common law married." I paused. "Either way, you might want to start making other arrangements."

She burst into tears again.

JD and I exchanged a glance.

"Do you mind if we look around?" JD asked.

"Sure. Go ahead."

There was a bedroom on either side of the living room. JD took one side of the house, and I took the other. I'm not really sure what we were looking for—anything that might shed some light on the situation. A cell phone, or laptop, could prove invaluable. I figured his cell phone was likely at the bottom of ocean, but I did find a laptop in the bedroom. I took it and stepped back into the living room. "Is this Scott's laptop, or yours?"

"It's Scott's. I don't have a computer. I just use my phone and my tablet."

"You mind if I borrow this for a few days. I swear I'll bring it back."

"Sure. If you think it will help?"

"Do you know the password?"

"No. Scott never told me any of his passwords. He kept his business to himself."

JD stepped back into the living room.

"Thanks for your help," I said as I left my number on the coffee table. "If you can think of anything else, let me know. And if you change residences, keep us informed. We might have more questions."

"I'm totally fucked," she cried. "I've got no place else to go. The only money I have is what's in our bank account, and a little bit of cash he's got stashed away around here."

"I'll see if I can put you in touch with an attorney," I said, feeling sorry for her.

We left the residence, and JD drove toward the Marina.

"What do you think?" I asked.

"I think her meal ticket just ran out." He thought about it for a moment. "But I don't think she killed him. Doesn't look like she had anything to gain by it. I'll see what I can find out about this *Carlos* guy. There can't be too many people that recently got released from Raiford with the name Carlos."

JD pulled a set of keys from his pocket. They weren't his. He had a devilish grin on his face.

"What's that?"

"Scott Kingston's keys."

"You can't take those," I admonished.

"Whoops. Too late. Now we can take a look around his office without having to break in."

"We're supposed to be playing by the rules now."

"Do you want to find out who killed Scott Kingston, or don't you?" Jack asked. "And I know a great little analyst that can probably hack that computer in no time."

Jack whisked us across town to his friend's house. It was a small bungalow not far from the beach. We parked the car on the circular drive and strolled to the door. He gave me a warning before we knocked. "She's really smart, cute as a button, and totally off-limits. I mean it. I don't want to screw up this contact."

I raised my hands, innocently. "I'm not the one who hits on everything that walks."

Jack knocked on the door and this cute little redhead with pigtails answered. She had a headset on and a game controller in her hand. She wore jean shorts and a tube top. She was totally geeky hot. "What do you want? I'm live-streaming right now."

"I need a favor," Jack said.

"Live-streaming?" I asked.

She looked at me like I was a moron. "I'm playing Assassin's Code."

"She's really good at it," JD added. "People pay to watch."

"Really?"

"Yes, really," Ashley said in an annoyed tone. "And I don't get tips when I'm not playing. So make it snappy."

"We need you to get into this computer, look around for account information, ledgers, surveillance footage," JD said.

"Who's your friend?" she asked, eying me curiously.

"He's good people," JD said. "Ashley, Tyson. Tyson, Ashley."

"Nice to meet you," I said.

She arched an eyebrow and said nothing. Then, without even considering it, "I don't really have time for this."

"Make time," JD said. "For me. Pretty please?"

She huffed and folded her arms. "Fine. But I'm billing you for lost revenue."

JD grumbled. "Deal." Then he added, "I need a receipt."

"Then I'm not giving you a cash discount," Ashly snottily replied.

"At least charge me *friend* prices?" JD pleaded.

She groaned.

"Hey, who bailed you out when you got busted for weed?"

"Okay, okay. *Friend* prices."

JD nodded to me, and I handed Ashley the computer. She closed the door in our faces as soon as she took the device.

"We need that ASAP," JD shouted through the door.

My eyes narrowed at Jack. "So, we just handed over our best piece of evidence to a gamer girl?"

"I'm telling you, she's the best hacker I know. She can get into any system, pull data from a wiped hard drive, you name it. She's impressive."

"How old is she?"

"19."

"Have you worked with her before?"

"The girl's done work for the CIA, NSA, Cobra Company, the Israelis, and Lord knows who else."

"And you trust her?"

"Implicitly. I've known her since she was a kid—a friend of Scarlett's."

"How long does she usually take?"

JD shrugged. "Depends on what kind of encryption Kingston has on that computer. She'll bypass the system password in no time. But if he's used an advanced encryption algorithm for any of his data, which he probably has, could be a day, a week, a month. Who know?"

We left Ashley's and JD dropped me off at *Diver Down*. "I'll call you after my lunch meeting."

"Lunch? What's her name?"

"Belinda." He cupped his hands in front of his chest, exaggerating the size of her assets. "Sweet girl.

"After all the grief you gave me about Aria?"

"A man's gotta do what a man's gotta do."

"How old is she?"

"23," he beamed with pride.

I shook my head. The girl was half his age.

Jack shrugged. He dropped the car into gear and sped away.

I sauntered down the dock toward the *Slick'n Salty*. It was turning out to be a nice day. The squawk of gulls echoed across the Marina and the boats gently rocked. I scaled the transom of the *Slick'n Salty* and pushed into the salon. I was hoping to peel off my clothes and get back in bed with Aria, but it was a little late for that.

Things didn't exactly go according to plan. I opened the hatch to my stateroom and my heart sank.

Aria was stuffing her clothes into a small carry-on rolling bag.

My face twisted, confused. "Going somewhere?"

A guilty look played on her face. She'd been caught red-handed. She cringed. "I'm going back to New York. I was kind of hoping to slip out while you were gone. I hate goodbyes."

My jaw dropped.

I usually had a pretty good read on people, and I wasn't expecting this. "New York? How long?"

"I don't know."

"Oh…" I said, realizing this was a permanent address change.

She moved close and hugged me, the way you'd hug a friend. "This is why I hate goodbyes. I'm no good at them."

"Then don't go," I said, wrapping my arms around her.

"I have to. I can't stay here forever. It's not that I don't love being with you. It's just that… I've been passing up so many modeling opportunities, and I I need to get back to the city."

My throat tightened. I liked this girl more than I wanted to admit. My heart pounded uncomfortably. "I understand."

"This doesn't mean we're not gonna see each other again."

"Sure," I said for lack of anything better to say.

"You're upset."

"No. I'm not upset," I lied.

"You know I love being with you. But I've been totally neglecting my career. I'm losing follower counts. I'm not getting as many offers."

"I totally get it. You need to do what you need to do." I forced the words out, trying to maintain my cool.

"I'm not really used to this whole *relationship* thing. I'm used to guys just not texting anymore when they're not interested."

"I never said I wasn't interested."

"I know," she said, quickly. "It's just, I'm no good at the whole break up thing."

"I thought you said we were still going to see each other?"

"Of course. But, I don't think we should try to do the *long distance* thing. I mean, it would create unrealistic expectations, and it wouldn't be fair to either of us. I mean, come on, you're a hot guy. You'll have another girl in your bed tomorrow."

I appreciated her vote of confidence, but I wasn't quite sure there would be someone else keeping my sheets warm that soon.

"Did you meet somebody else?" I had to ask. It was eating away at me. I knew better than to ask that question, but I couldn't resist.

"Oh my God no. Of course not." She lifted on her tiptoes and kissed me passionately. Her full lips melted into mine, and her warm body felt amazing pressed against me. "Believe me, I hate that I have to leave. But, you know, my career is not going to last forever. These tits aren't always going to defy gravity. I need to make the most out of this while I've got it."

"Something tells me you're going to defy gravity for a long time."

She kissed me again. "I should get going. I booked a flight out at 1:30.

I looked at my watch. "Plenty of time to get in one last hurrah..."

She arched an intrigued eyebrow at me. Then smiled. "I guess I've got enough time."

6

The boat felt empty after Aria left.

So did my heart.

I had this strange sensation like something had been ripped from my insides. I was usually excellent about separating my emotions—putting things in little compartments and locking them away where I would never have to acknowledge them again. But I had let myself get closer to her than I should have.

No big deal.

It was time to put on my big boy pants and accept the fact that I got dumped. Nothing a little whiskey and another woman couldn't fix. *At least, that's what I told myself.*

Aria had taken an Uber to the airport. She said she'd call or text when she made it back to New York. I was pretty sure I would never see her again. She lived a fast-paced life, and I was a little surprised she slowed down a few weeks for me.

I told JD all about the situation when he called. He filled me with the usual words of encouragement, saying something about getting back on the horse. "The best way to get over someone is to get on top of someone else."

It all made sense, but it did little to fill the empty pit in my stomach.

"So, how did things go with Belinda?" I asked.

"It went well. She laughed at my stupid jokes. That's a good sign. Right? We're gonna meet up for drinks later. I'm sure she's got a few hot friends if you want to tag along?"

"I think I'm going to sit out for a few innings. Catch my breath."

"That's a mistake. You need to get another *at-bat*, slugger. I'll swing by and pick you up in a little bit. I tracked down Travis Wilkes. I think we should pay him a little visit."

"Roger that."

I hung up, pulled my sorry ass out of bed, and sauntered down the dock toward *Diver Down*. I had pretty much lost my appetite. But I figured a cheeseburger and a beer might give me an attitude adjustment. I took a seat at the end of the bar and ordered.

Madison looked at me, confused. "Where's Aria?"

I grimaced and told her the situation.

"Are you sure you're not the one who dumped her?" she asked.

"I'm pretty sure about that."

"Really? That's not your style."

"I'm not the insensitive monster you make me out to be."

She looked at me with skeptical eyes. "Well, I'm sorry to hear that. I liked her."

"So did I."

She made a sad face. "Aw, big brother's got a broken heart. Serves you right."

I scowled at her.

She was still pissed because I dumped her friend Hannah. It's not that I *dumped* her. More like, I pushed her away. It was for her own good. At least, that's how I justified it at the time.

JD showed up when I was halfway through my burger. He ordered one for himself and another round of beer. "Put it on his tab," he said, pointing to me.

"His tab is getting pretty big," Madison said, giving me the side-eye.

"I'm good for it," I replied.

"How's it going, JD?" Madison asked.

"I can't complain."

"How's Scarlett?"

JD groaned. "Okay, maybe I can complain. That little hellion just started dating this loser, Justin Meeks."

"Oh, I know him," Madison said. "He doesn't seem like a bad kid."

"He's got a slick exterior, but he's trouble. Let me tell you."

"Really, Jack?" she said, dryly.

"Believe me, I know trouble when I see it."

"What's the matter? Worried she met someone like you?" Madison asked.

Jack scoffed. "He ain't nothing like me. That kid is a bad influence."

Madison rolled her eyes. "She's 18, Jack. You don't have a say in the matter anymore."

"As long as she's living under my roof, I've got a say in the matter. If that boyfriend of hers ain't careful, I'm gonna carve him up and feed him to the sharks."

"Take a deep breath," Madison said. "I don't want you to have a heart attack in my bar."

JD was getting a little red in the face, and the veins in his neck were starting to bulge. It was a little amusing to see him get so worked up.

"I just get so goddamn mad at her. She's got no common sense. She comes and goes whenever she pleases, stays out all hours of the night, burns through every penny she makes at that shitty waitressing job, and she still hasn't enrolled in school."

"Go easy on the waitresses," Madison said.

"I wouldn't get too worked up about it," I said. "She'll be onto another guy in two weeks."

JD arched an eyebrow at me. "Are you saying my daughter gets around?"

"You know what I meant. She's got the attention span of a gnat. She'll lose interest in the guy in no time. Trust me."

"I hope you're right."

JD inhaled his cheeseburger. It was like the man was starving.

"Didn't you just eat lunch?"

"She had a salad. Which pretty much meant I could only eat a salad. So, no, I wouldn't call that lunch."

After JD finished, I asked for the check to settle my tab. "Are you still offering a discount to law enforcement?"

"Yep. LEOs don't pay around here."

A shit-eating grin curled on my lips. I exchanged a glance with JD, then flashed my gold badge. "I guess this one's on the house?"

Madison's astonished face crinkled with contempt. "What is this bullshit?"

She grabbed the badge and surveyed it closely. "Did you buy this at a novelty shop?" she said, half joking, not wanting to believe it.

"Nope," I said, still grinning.

"Who in their right mind would deputize you two?"

"Sheriff Daniels knows talent when he sees it," I said.

She scoffed. "The only talent you two dipshits have is being annoying. You both excel at that!"

"Don't hate," I said.

"New rule. Free meals for law enforcement officers that aren't either of you."

I scowled at her playfully and settled up my full tab which had been growing over the last week.

We left *Diver Down* and headed over to the *Pirate's Cove* marina. The slip where Wilkes's boat should have been docked was empty. The only person around was a guy on a neighboring boat, cleaning fish.

"Excuse me, do you have any idea where we could find Travis Wilkes?" I asked.

"If his boat's not here, he's probably out on the water," the man said in a snide tone.

"Really? I hadn't considered that," I snarked.

He looked up from his fish and glared at us. "Who's asking?"

I let JD flash his badge because I knew he wanted to.

The man suddenly changed his tune. "He took some girls out. I think he said he was going down to Black Rock Key. But don't quote me on that."

"Thanks," I said.

"Want to track them down?" JD asked. "We can probably get there in an hour. Be a good excuse to get out on the water. We can expense the fuel." He grinned.

"Sure. Why not?"

We headed back to the marina at *Diver Down* and boarded the *Slick'n Salty*. Jack cranked up the engines and idled us out of the harbor. He throttled up and brought the boat on plane, skimming across the ocean.

It was a beautiful day, and the wind raced through my hair. The seas were calm, and the sun's reflection glimmered on the water.

This was definitely the life.

When we arrived at Black Rock Key, it wasn't hard to spot Travis Wilkes's boat. The thing was a behemoth—a 65 foot luxury yacht named *The Good Life*. It has a sticker on the stern that read: *My other boat's a piece of shit too*.

It had sleek lines and graceful curves. And I'm not just talking about the boat. There were several scantily clad women on board, sunning themselves topless. Music blasted from the stereo, and a deckhand served cocktails.

The party was in full swing.

We pulled alongside *The Good Life* and dropped anchor.

"Mind if we join you?" JD shouted.

"The more the merrier," a stunning blonde replied.

We boarded the boat and joined the festivities.

"Know where I could find Travis?" I asked the blonde.

She pointed toward the salon with a smile. I tried not to ogle her jiggling bare breasts. *Let's just say it was extremely difficult to pry my eyes away.* They were absolutely perfect.

"On top of another," JD said, patting my back with a grin, encouraging me to get back on the horse. "On top of another."

I focused my attention on the task at hand.

Travis was not a looker. His pudgy belly hung over the waistline of his board-shorts. He had a fat head, narrow eyes, and looked like he may have been dropped as a child. But apparently he'd done well for himself in the tech industry. He sat on a sofa and sparked up a fat joint as we entered the salon.

JD flashed his badge again, making Travis grimace.

"Oh, come on, man! You're not gonna bust me for a little joint, are you?"

"Not if you answer a few questions," JD said, throwing his weight around.

"I'm not answering any questions without my lawyer."

"You don't even know what this is about," I said.

"I don't need to. Talking to cops is always a bad idea."

"It's about Scott Kingston."

"Fuck that guy."

"So, I take it you didn't get along?" I said.

"That ass-clown fucked my girlfriend."

Two stunning beauties pawed at him from either side.

"Looks like it worked out okay for you," JD said.

"It's the principle of the thing," Travis said. He took a drag on the joint and blew the smoke in JD's face.

"I guess that gives you motive to kill the guy," JD said.

"What are you talking about?"

"Kingston washed up on the shore this morning with two bullets to the back of the head," I said.

"Couldn't have happened to a nicer guy."

"You own a gun, Mr. Wilkes?" I asked.

"Fuck you both. I'm not saying another word."

"Is your girlfriend around? We'd like to speak with her," JD said.

"I kicked that stupid bitch to the curb."

"What's her name?" I asked.

"Like I said. I'm not saying anything without my attorney."

"It would be a shame to ruin your party and bust you for possession. You might have to forfeit the boat," JD said.

"Yeah. That would hurt. Wouldn't it?" I said.

"I paid 6 million for this boat. You can't take it over a joint."

"I believe we can," JD said. He had no idea what he was talking about, but it sure as hell made Wilkes nervous.

"We'd be inclined to forget all about this if you just answered a few questions," I said. "I mean, if you didn't kill Kingston, you've got nothing to worry about."

Wilkes glared at us with his red, glassy eyes as he pondered things.

7

"Riley Johnson," Travis said. "That's my ex. Go talk to her. Skank. I'm sure she's going to say all kinds of terrible things about me. But I didn't kill Kingston. When did you say he died? Three weeks ago? I wasn't even in the country then. I was in Monaco, banging some hot ass bitches, I might add."

"Can you prove that you were out of the country?" I asked.

"I didn't fly commercial. I chartered my own plane. Want to see the receipts? I didn't kill the guy." He paused. "Sure, I may have sent him some threatening texts. But he was a peon. Not worth my time. It's not like I gave a shit about Riley, anyway. It was the point of the thing. Kingston took something that was mine."

"We'll check out your story," JD said.

"Don't leave town until we've cleared you," I added.

He glared at us. "If you're done, I'd like you to get the fuck off my boat."

"Sure thing," I said.

JD and I strolled out of the salon, straddled the gunwale, and boarded the *Slick'n Salty*. We weighed anchor, and JD cranked up the engines, leaving the bouncing beauties behind.

"He sure has a pleasant disposition," I said.

"The guy's all talk. He couldn't have killed Kingston himself. But he might have paid someone to do it."

"And he was conveniently out of the country at the time."

"Let's talk to the girlfriend," JD said. "Get her side of the story."

We made our way back to the marina, and by the time we hooked up water and power, Special Agent Archer was sauntering down the dock. She flashed a bright smile, and her perfect teeth sparkled in the late afternoon sun. She had a smile that could sell toothpaste. "Afternoon, boys."

"Agent Archer," I said, courteously. I sat on the gunwale in the cockpit. "What can I do for you?"

"I think we got off on the wrong foot. I've got some information that I think you boys might find useful."

"Oh, so you've come bearing gifts, and you think you can get into our good graces?" JD said.

She shrugged. "Something like that."

"What have you got?" I asked.

"I pulled Kingston's phone records. He had a number of threatening texts from a number that is registered to—"

"Travis Wilkes," I said, cutting her off.

She frowned.

I smiled. "You're going to have to do better than that."

She bit her lip in the most adorable way as she thought about what else she could offer.

"Looking cute's not going to cut it," I said.

"Speak for yourself," JD muttered.

She let out an annoyed sigh, and her cheeks flushed with embarrassment. She barked, "I am not cute, Mr. Wild!"

"Well, I wouldn't call you ugly. At least, not after a few beers." I was trying to get a rise out of her, and it was working.

The vein that ran down the middle of her forehead started to pulse, and her face grew even redder. She folded her arms and bit her tongue, trying to contain herself. "Perhaps you don't want my assistance now, but I'm sure there may come a time when you need the resources the FBI has to offer. Good afternoon, gentlemen."

She spun around and strutted away.

JD and I watched her mesmerizing assets as they swung from side to side.

"Agent Archer," I yelled, stopping her midway down the dock.

She paused for a moment before turning around, lifting a perturbed eyebrow at the two of us.

"How about I buy you dinner, and we can talk about the case?" I suggested.

"Dinner?"

I raised my hands innocently. "A free exchange of information."

"A free exchange of bodily fluids," JD muttered in my ear.

"Just information," she said, adamantly.

"I'll show you mine if you show me yours," I said with a grin.

She rolled her eyes.

I scaled the transom and trotted down the dock, catching up with her.

JD followed.

We grabbed a table at *Diver Down* and ordered a bucket of beer.

Kim waited on us. She had platinum blonde hair, pulled back in a ponytail. She was 19 and taking the year off from school.

JD pulled an amber bottle out of the bucket of ice and twisted the top. A blast of air escaped. He took a swig of the cold brew, and I grabbed a bottle and offered one to Archer.

She passed. "Do you two always drink on the job?"

JD looked at his watch and grinned. "We are off duty."

"Are you two ever really on duty?" She asked.

"I don't know," JD said. "We just got deputized this morning, so not much of a track record."

Archer just shook her head. "What did you find out from Wilkes?"

I gave her a brief synopsis. "You can do us a favor. Verify he was actually in Monaco during the time of the murder. Check his accounts for any unusual transactions during that time."

"I'd need a warrant for that."

I scoffed.

"Hey, some of us play by the rules," Archer said. "Have you got anything else?"

"A few leads that we need to look into, but nothing substantial," I said.

"What about you?" JD asked.

"Not much. And it seems you know everything I know, so..."

"What's your angle on this?" I asked.

"I don't have an angle," Archer replied.

"Everybody's got an angle," I said, dryly.

"What's *your* angle?" she replied.

"JD and I are concerned citizens." I smiled.

She rolled her eyes again.

"You can't possibly be interested in the death of a boat dealer unless there is something more under the surface," I said.

She chose her words carefully. "It's no secret he had a lot of dealings with some less than reputable people. I want to know why he was killed, and by whom. I'd like to see if it somehow plays into the broader picture."

"What broader picture?" I asked.

She hesitated a moment. "Do you know how much cocaine has been seized this year by the Coast Guard?"

I shrugged. "I don't know. 150,000 pounds?"

"Close. 167,000 pounds," she said. "And we're only capturing a small percentage of what comes through. We don't know the real number. But it's probably about 2% of the total. That means 98% is slipping through unaccounted for."

"You're never going to be able to stop it," I said.

"So, why bother, right?"

I shrugged.

"This stuff destroys lives," Archer said. "I've seen firsthand what addiction does."

"I get it," I said. "You want to make a difference. We all do. But the only reason the cartels are bringing this in by the boatload is because there is a demand for it. We artificially prop up prices with our failed drug policy, and violence results from the high-stakes."

"So, your solution is to legalize it?" Archer asked, pointedly.

"I'm not a politician. I don't provide solutions. I'm just saying, maybe we need to re-evaluate the way we do things?"

"Have you seen what this stuff does to kids? How would you feel if you had a daughter who was strung out on this stuff? Or did *things* to get her fix?"

"My daughter's no saint, but she's smart enough to stay away from that kind of trouble," JD said.

"Some girls don't have a choice. They meet a guy, they fall in love, the guy gets them hooked on smack, and the next thing you know, she's turning tricks for him."

JD grew uncomfortable. "Okay. Stop. I don't need to hear anymore. I thought this was going to be a casual dinner."

"Sounds like this is personal to you," I said.

"It is," Archer replied.

I didn't press the issue, but I could see behind her eyes that somebody close to her had gone down the wrong path—and the scabs were still raw. "So what's your point? We are obviously not going to fix the world's problems over dinner."

She took a deep breath, and I could see that she was deciding how much she should say. "You're right. I can't stop all of it. But I can at least make sure we're not helping. Are you familiar with the Muerte Dolorosa cartel out of Columbia?"

I nodded.

"They are one of the largest traffickers of cocaine and heroin. Yet there hasn't been a seizure of one of their shipments in the past year. Either they are really lucky, or they're getting inside assistance."

8

"You think law enforcement is involved?" I asked.

"Yep," Archer said. Her eyes blazed into me. "Either someone at the local level, or within the Joint Interagency Task Force itself. Coast Guard? Customs and Border Patrol? I don't know."

"I bet that makes you pretty popular," JD said.

"I've run into my fair share of opposition. But I can handle myself."

"Well, if you think JD and I have anything to do with drug smuggling, you're barking up the wrong tree," I said.

"What about your boss?" Archer asked.

"You can't be serious?" JD grumbled. "Wayne Daniels? Not possible."

"Hey, I'm just trying to leave no stone unturned."

"If you think we're going to snitch for you, you are sadly mistaken," JD said.

"I'm not looking for a snitch. I'm looking for anything that will lead me to the truth," Agent Archer said. "And I don't care where it leads."

"I can see that," JD said.

"I was hoping something might turn up with this *Kingston* case. He obviously had the connections, and no doubt leased boats to Muerte Dolorosa members. All I'm asking is that you keep me informed if you turn up anything that you think I might find of interest."

JD and I exchanged a glance.

"I don't see a problem with that," I said.

Archer smiled. "Good. So we're all on the same team."

She looked at her watch. "I guess I'm off duty now." She grabbed a beer from the bucket and twisted the top.

My phone buzzed in my pocket. I pulled it out and looked at the caller ID. Isabella.

Decline.

"Is that important?" Archer asked. "Do you need to take that?"

"No," I lied.

Kim returned to take our order. JD ordered the soft-shell crab. I was craving a bowl of lobster bisque. Agent Archer opted for the fried shrimp.

The meal was excellent.

By the time we finished, JD's phone was blowing up. He exchanged half a dozen messages with somebody, then shoveled the last bits of his softshell crab in his mouth. "I hate to eat and run, but booty, I mean duty, calls."

I raised a curious eyebrow. "Belinda?"

"She wants to meet for cocktails." JD's eyes sparkled with excitement. "Are you sure you don't want to tag along? I can tell her to bring some hot friends."

"No, thanks. I'm fine."

"Don't let me keep you from anything," Archer said.

"You're not keeping me from anything," I said.

JD put his napkin on the table and stood up. "This one's on you, right?"

"I've got it," I said.

"We talked about business, so we can expense it."

"I don't think we can expense it if we're not getting paid."

"Out of pocket expenses." He said goodbye to Agent Archer and dashed out the door.

"He is quite the character," Archer said.

"That he is."

"Are you sure I'm not keeping you from anything?" It was almost like she was fishing.

"You like blues music?"

Archer shrugged. "I guess."

"There's a guy playing over at *The Crazy Conch* tonight. He's Stevie Ray reincarnated."

She looked at me, confused. "Who's Stevie Ray?"

I dropped my head in my hands and shook it with disbelief. "Only one of the greatest blues guitar players of all time."

"Aren't all blues songs sort of the same?"

"That's beside the point. I mean, you could say the same thing about all pop songs."

She conceded that fact. "Are you buying the drinks?"

"Sure."

"Count me in. We'll call it research."

"You're driving," I said.

She shook her head. "I don't drink and drive."

"You had two beers?"

"I'm not doing anything to jeopardize my position. I worked too hard to get here. That's a 60 day suspension without pay."

"So, you're a risk taker?" I said, dryly.

"Funny," she groaned.

We caught an Uber over to *The Crazy Conch*. It was like most of the bars in Coconut Key—thatched roofs, bamboo, and tiki torches. Jimmy Dale Watson could certainly shred on guitar. He had tone for days and had a gravelly voice that could sing just about anything with an extra heaping of heart and soul.

He was as good as any of the great guitar players in history. The sad thing was he had 4000 followers on Facebook, hustled CDs after the show, and barely made enough from the gig to get to the next town.

The Crazy Conch had a pretty laid-back vibe. There was usually a mix of tourists and regulars. Old timers that sat at the bar all day long and would look at you funny if you took a seat next to them. Without fail, every time I was here, there was a guy on roller skates dancing to the music. He twirled around for a few songs by himself, then skated out the door and onto another bar.

The sun was down, and I decided to switch to whiskey. We sat at a cocktail table and took in the sights and sounds.

"How long have you been in Coconut Key?" I asked.

"Six months," Archer said. "This is my first assignment out of the academy. I put it as number one on my wish list, and I got it."

"Why this?"

She hesitated for a moment. "My sister started doing drugs at 16. Got hooked up with the wrong crowd. She was trafficked, strung out, and dead by 19."

That hung in the air.

"I'm sorry."

Her eyes grew slick. "Yeah, me too. But I swore I would do everything I could to keep that from happening to another girl."

"An admirable goal."

She quickly changed the subject. "So, the band is not bad. Not totally my thing, but I can dig it."

"Not bad? Not bad? It's *Jimmy Dale Watson!* Trust me, some-day, you'll be telling your grandkids that you saw him in some dive bar when he was nobody."

She looked at me with a healthy dose of skepticism. "Doubtful."

"What? Not planning on having grandkids?"

She laughed. "Slow down. I haven't even gotten to the *kids* part."

There was an awkward pause.

"You got any kids?" she asked. "Ex-wives?"

"Nope."

"Want any?"

"Kids, or ex-wives?"

She chuckled. "Well, hopefully when you commit, it's for life."

I shivered. "That's terrifying."

"One of *those*, are you?"

"I have no problem with commitment. I just haven't found a situation I want to commit to." I smiled.

She scowled at me playfully.

"But I think someday I'd like to have kids. Settle down. Have a nice family. Have someone to take care of me when I get old and can't remember my name."

"So, you want kids for purely selfish reasons?"

"No. I didn't say that... Besides, at the rate I'm going, I'm not going to live long enough to get old, anyway."

"What makes you say that?"

I shrugged. "This is Coconut Key. I could wash up on the beach with two bullets in the back of my head. This place is turning out to be more dangerous than some combat zones I've been in."

She let out a resigned sigh of agreement.

We ordered another round of drinks and talked some more. I stuck with whiskey, and she stuck with margaritas. I forgot to warn her that they were pretty lethal here. She stood up to go to the bathroom and fell back into her seat. "Whoops," she slurred.

I rushed to help her as she tried to stand again. I took hold of her arm and steadied her.

"I think I might have exceeded my limit."

"Don't feel bad. They creep up on you here."

"I can see that." She took a minute to get her bearings. "Is the Earth moving, or is that just me?"

"That's just you."

"I'm going to attempt to navigate my way to the little girl's room. Then I'm gonna go home. Thank you for the drinks."

"Hang on, I'll help you get there."

"I can do it on my own." She took a few steps, then stumbled.

I caught her before she fell. "I think you definitely need navigational assistance."

I helped her to the ladies' room, then asked a woman waiting in line to give her a hand.

Archer was in there for a long time, and I started to get worried about her. I was about to call in reinforcements, when she emerged, looking like she'd been through the ringer.

"You don't drink much, do you?"

"Not *this* much," she slurred. "I'm fine now. I worshiped at the altar, tithed, and everything is *A-okay*."

She looked far from okay.

I took her arm and escorted her through the bar. We caught an Uber back to her house, and she passed out along the way.

I scooped her out of the car and carried her in my arms to her front door. I revived her long enough for her to fumble for her keys.

15 minutes later we actually entered the foyer.

She kicked off her heels and staggered to her bedroom, peeling off the layers of her pantsuit. Her navy jacket hit the floor, then her pants, then her blouse. I tried not to look.

She face-planted on her bed and was out cold.

I tucked a pillow under her head and covered her up. I grabbed another pillow and moved to the couch in the living room and set the alarm on my watch to check on her. I didn't want her choking on her own vomit in the middle of the night.

She had a nice little place with an ocean view. The home was cozy and tidy. This was a girl who had everything squared away. The fridge and the pantry were nice and organized. I wasn't snooping, but I needed some midnight rations—especially since I was on *fire-watch*.

I snacked on a protein bar and milk, then curled up on the couch. It was the first time I slept on dry land in a long while. It took a little getting used to, without the gentle rocking of the boat.

Soon after I nodded off, my phone buzzed again. At first I thought it was my alarm, but it was Isabella calling.

I reluctantly swiped the screen to answer.

9

"You've been avoiding me," Isabella said.

"I've been busy," I replied.

"This is urgent."

"What is it?"

"We have a situation. And you are in the middle of it."

"What's going on?"

"Your little FBI friend is causing problems for our client."

My eyes perked up. "What are you talking about?"

"Do you think I don't have eyes on you?"

I sighed. Isabella had operatives and watchers all over the globe.

"Muerte Dolorosa is off-limits. they have an agreement with our client. They get to operate hassle free in exchange for their cooperation with Operation Red Storm."

"Operation Red Storm?"

"If you haven't noticed, there is about to be a power vacuum in Venezuela—if all goes well. It is in our best interest to have the right leadership installed. The cartel is supplying rebels with weapons and funding, and the CIA is actively involved in PSYOPS. I don't need to tell you that we can't have the FBI looking at Muerte Dolorosa stateside and gathering evidence that could connect the CIA."

"So, that's how the cartel is moving shipments in and out and avoiding law enforcement?"

"I need you to deal with the situation," Isabella said, dryly.

"What exactly do you mean by *deal with the situation?*" I knew what she meant.

"Do I need to spell it out for you?"

"That's a *big* ask." I got off the couch and quietly slipped through the sliding glass doors, onto the patio, and closed them behind me.

"It could be a big problem if this gets exposed," Isabella said.

I whispered, "So you want me to obstruct justice and interfere with federal investigation?"

"No. I want you to get rid of the problem."

"No."

"I'm sorry. I didn't hear you."

"I said no."

"You can't say no."

"I just did."

"You owe me," Isabella said in a stern tone.

That hung there for a moment.

As cold and as calculated as this woman was, Isabella had saved my ass and provided valuable intel when JD's daughter had been kidnapped. I was trying to put my days with Cobra Company behind me, but I had given her my word I would return the favor.

Cobra Company provided plausible deniability to their clients. It was made up of former spooks and spec-war operators. They'd grown into a force to be reckoned with—a shadow intelligence agency with elite warriors that could be deployed at a moments notice without congressional approval or oversight.

"If you won't do the job, I will send someone who will. This is non-negotiable, and our client won't take no for an answer."

I paused for a long moment. "If you send someone else to do the job, I guarantee you, they will end up in a body bag."

"Now that's the Tyson that I know and love."

"I will steer her in another direction."

"That's not what I asked you to do."

"Assure the client she won't be a problem."

"You know as well as I do they like to deal with absolutes."

"I'll take care of it. But nothing happens to her. Got it?"

"Dinner and a few drinks, and you're already whooped? Should I be worried about you?"

"Trust me. I'm saving you, and our client, from a bigger headache. If she magically disappears, there will be another agent to take her place. And more questions will be asked."

"Have you ever considered psychological counseling? Might help work through some of these issues you have?"

"I have issues?"

"A killer who doesn't want to kill? I'd say you have a few hangups."

"I'm not a killer anymore."

"Sure you're not." She hung up the phone.

I gritted my teeth, and my hands balled into fists. I grumbled to myself for a moment, before slipping back inside and trying to get a little sleep on the couch.

I was too wound up.

Morning came too soon, especially for Agent Archer. She staggered out of her bedroom, wiping her eyes, her hair tousled, still wearing nothing but her bra and panties. She shrieked when she saw me on the couch and covered herself with her hands. "What the hell are you doing here?"

"I take it you don't remember last night?"

Her bloodshot eyes narrowed at me "We didn't do anything, did we?"

I laughed. "Oh, I could have a lot of fun with this, but, no, nothing happened."

She looked relieved. "The last thing I remember is listening to a blues band and drinking really strong margaritas."

"I'll spare you the details from that point on."

"Oh, no." I could see glimpses of the previous night flash across her brain.

"I brought you home, and I thought I'd better stay with you just to make sure you didn't die like a rock star."

"Thank you," she said cringing with embarrassment.

She's shuffled back into her room, not wanting to turn around and expose her backside, which I had already seen —and it was delicious.

She emerged a few moments later wearing pajamas. "I'd fix you breakfast, but I need to get the hell out of here. I'm running late."

"No problem. I'll take a rain check."

"You can sleep in, if you want. Just lock up when you leave." She disappeared back into the bedroom and slipped into the shower.

I swear to God, I've never seen a woman get ready so fast before in my life. She emerged from the bedroom 20 minutes later wearing a dark gray pantsuit, with her makeup done, her hair pulled back in a bun, and a pair of sunglasses in her hands.

"Have a great day, sweetie," I said, in a sardonic tone.

She flipped me off and strolled out of the door.

I got up, found a bagel in the fridge, slathered cream cheese on it and called an Uber.

As I left the house, I ran into a kid walking up the driveway.

He was maybe 17 or 18. Short blond hair, fresh face. "Is Jen around?"

"No, she just left for work."

"Okay. Tell her Tommy stopped by. She wanted me to look at her car."

"I'll tell her."

We chatted for a few moments as I waited for my Uber. His dad ran a local repair shop in town. "So, you're Earl's kid?"

"Yes, sir."

"How's he doing?"

"Good."

"He used to service my dad's cars. Tell him Tyler Wild says hello."

"I will."

Back at the Slick'n Salty, I took a shower and got changed, then called JD. "We should probably talk to Riley Johnson today. Travis's girlfriend."

"Sounds good. Give me about an hour."

"How did it go with Belinda last night?"

"Dude... Unbelievable. The things she can do with her... That girl is on fire. I'm telling you. You missed out. She's got some hot little friends, too."

"Maybe next time."

"How did it go with Agent Archer?"

"I'll tell you all about it later."

It was just before noon by the time we arrived at *Forbidden Fruit*—a strip club on the west side of Coconut Key. Needless to say, JD was in his element.

A flash of our golden badges gained us access without paying a cover charge. It was a little early for deep thundering based music, but the visual scenery more than made up for it. Spotlights slashed the hazy air. There were three stages with mirrored floors and ceilings. Scantily clad beauties performed acrobatic maneuvers around glimmering poles, showcasing toned legs, stiletto heels, and gravity defying curves.

"Jasmine, Stage II. Jasmine, Stage II," the DJ said in a low radio announcer voice.

JD knew the manager and half the girls in the place. The manager pointed to Riley Johnson, who went by the stage name Cherry Bomb. Her hips were undulating on Stage III, and every man in the place was jealous of the pole.

"She came back to work after she broke up with Travis," the manager said. "Maybe four or five weeks now? I'm not sure. The days all run together around here." He paused "Try not to flash your badges around here. It makes the customers, and the girls, nervous. Why don't you head back to one of the VIP rooms, and I'll send Cherry over."

He tapped an earbud that allowed him to communicate with the staff. "We have any rooms open?"

A bouncer crackled back in his ear.

I couldn't hear anything over the music.

"Take room six," the manager said to us a moment later.

He pointed to a bouncer that was standing by a velvet rope which led into an exclusive area.

JD thanked the manager, and we strolled to the VIP lounge like rock stars. The velvet rope opened for us, and we walked to room number six.

The rooms were decorated like a cheap motel room in Vegas. There was a couch, a bed, a pole on a small stage, and mirrors on the ceiling. There were lava lamps on the night-stands, and the lighting was dim and sultry.

"Okay, I can safely say I have never been in one of these rooms before with another dude," JD said.

It was a bit awkward.

Cherry strutted into the room a few minutes later. "Eddie said you wanted to talk to me?"

She had platinum blonde hair, stiletto heels, fishnet stockings, frilly panties, and a lacy garter belt. She was clasping her push-up bra as she entered.

JD had a hard time maintaining focus.

"We'd like to talk to you about Travis Wilkes." I said.

She groaned. "Ugh. I can't stand that guy. What a loser. Small dick."

"Thanks for the info, but what can you tell me about his relationship with Scott Kingston?" I asked.

"What do you want to know?"

"When was the last time you talk to Scott?"

She shrugged. "I don't know. We hooked up a few times. It was fun. I liked him, I guess. But, we just stopped texting each other. You know how it goes. I moved on to something else, and I assumed he did too. Why?"

I told her Scott was dead.

Her jaw dropped, and her eyes widened. She seemed genuinely shocked by the news. She asked how it happened.

I gave her as much of the details as I thought necessary. She didn't have enough of a connection to him to break down into tears. But she certainly didn't seem happy about the news.

"Do you think Travis killed him?" I asked.

She thought about it hard for a moment. "No. Travis talks a good game, but that's about it."

"Do you think he could have hired someone to do the job?"

"Why would Travis go to all that trouble over me?"

I shrugged. "He seemed pretty pissed off about the whole thing."

Riley rolled her eyes. "Please. I was just another fuck-toy for him. We were on the verge of breaking up anyway. And it's not like he could keep it in his pants. He always had plenty of options. There was always some girl wanting to ride the gravy train."

"What about Scott?" I asked. "Can you think of anybody that might have wanted him dead?"

"Scott didn't exactly run with an innocent crowd, if you

know what I mean," Riley said. "He did business with every drug dealer and Mafia boss from here to Medellin."

I gave her my number and told her to call me if she thought of anything that might be useful.

"Hey, do you think you can help me out with some parking tickets?"

JD smiled. "I'm sure I can help you with that."

Riley perked up. "That would be great. Maybe we can work out some kind of trade?"

JD practically salivated at her sultry offer.

He leaned over and muttered in my ear, "Would you mind stepping outside for a minute?"

I shook my head and strolled toward the door.

"You know, come to think of it," Riley said, "Scott owed some guy a lot of money. Scarpelli, Scaramelli—"

"Scarpetti?" I said.

"Yeah, that's it!"

"He was kinda nervous about it. I think it was a *lot* of money."

"Thanks. That's helpful."

She smiled. "You're welcome." Then she said in an innocently naughty voice, "So, is he the only one that can help me with my parking tickets, or could both of you lend a hand?"

10

I left the parking enforcement negotiations to JD and waited in the VIP lounge. He emerged from the room 15 minutes later with a wide smile. Riley slipped out of the room behind him adjusting her frilly unmentionables. She kissed JD on the cheek. "Thanks, sugar," she said, before disappearing back into the main area.

"That was quick," I said.

"What can I say? The girl gets paid by the hour. And she didn't have *that* many tickets."

I gave him a look.

"What? She just gave me a few dances."

"We need to talk to Scarpetti," I said. "But I guarantee you, he didn't kill Kingston."

"Why not?"

"You don't kill someone who owes you money. That's a good way to make sure you never get paid. You rough them up.

You break a few fingers. Break a few bones. But you don't put two bullets in the back of their skull unless you know they don't have the money. Kingston was the kind of guy who had access to large sums of cash. He could get his hands on whatever he owed. It might be uncomfortable. And he might have needed to shift a few things around. But under threat of death, he would've come up with it."

"I think we should definitely talk to him," JD said.

"By all means. I get the impression that not a lot happens on this island that he doesn't know about."

We stayed at *Forbidden Fruit* and chowed on the lunch buffet. It wasn't the greatest thing in the world. There were chicken fingers, buffalo wings, processed hamburgers, and pizza, which had probably been frozen at one point in time.

But people didn't come here for the cuisine.

JD and I watched with amusement as a high roller tossed money onto the stage like it were paper. Green bills fluttered through the air, falling like confetti around hourglass figures and toned legs.

The guy had money to burn.

He had a wide grin on his face, which was outshined by the smiles of the girls he showered with affection.

He had short blond hair and steely eyes and looked like he could have been a heavyweight boxer. He was dressed casually, wearing a T-shirt and board shorts. If you saw him on the street, you'd think he was your average tourist. And maybe he *was*. But tourists didn't travel with bodyguards. He had two stocky men nearby at all times. I gathered that under their suit jackets were semiautomatic pistols.

The guy liked to make a splash, and it was hard not to notice the cash raining down on the stage, and the girls scooping it up like addicts.

"Get a load of that cat," JD said.

"Who the hell is that?"

JD shrugged. He waved over the manager and inquired about *Mr. Spendy*.

"That's Vladimir Kazakov. Some kind of Russian tycoon. Obviously, we like him around here."

"Regular?"

"Fairly. Why are you asking?"

JD shrugged, innocently. "Just curious."

"Do not go harassing my good customers."

"I would do no such thing," JD said.

"He's harmless. He comes in here and throws money around and invites the girls onto his yacht. What kind of arrangement they work out with him, I don't know. I don't want to know." Then he added, "That's a tree you don't want to go barking up."

"Why not?" JD asked.

"He's tight with the mayor. Made a healthy campaign contribution. He's got a scholarship fund for economically challenged kids. And he just made a large endowment to some pediatric cancer foundation."

"Sounds like an upstanding member of the community. Except for a few indulgences, here and there," JD said.

"You're one to talk," the manager snarked. "He's a gravy train for a lot of people. Don't screw that up, JD."

JD raised his hands, innocently.

We left and headed to Kingston's marina. Dozens of luxury yachts were docked in slips. JD's eyes sparkled with desire. This is going to be one hell of an estate sale," JD said.

I scanned the area as we strolled down the dock toward the main office. JD used the keys he lifted from Kingston's place to open the door and we stepped inside.

It was an upscale place with expensive Italian furniture. There was a vending machine with free water and soda and snacks. There was a large flatscreen display, a lounge area, a reception desk, a sales office, Scott's personal office, and a conference room. There was a demo area for aftermarket stereo components that you could have installed in your luxury yacht as well as home theater options.

"What are we looking for?" JD asked.

"Surveillance footage, transaction ledgers, anything that might provide a little insight," I said.

I had noticed cameras on our way in. JD and I searched for the footage. It was probably stored on a computer or on the Internet somewhere, but all the desktop computers had been removed.

There was a restaurant with a patio next door that had a clear view of the marina.

"Maybe somebody saw something," I postulated.

"You think he was abducted here, taken on the water, and shot?"

"There's a good possibility. Until we can get access to his ledgers and accounts, we won't know if there are any boats missing from the marina. Did he have an assistant?"

"Scott worked by himself," JD said. "He was a one-man show. I don't think he wanted anyone getting too close to his business."

We went next door to the Cranky Crab. It was a restaurant bar with a large wooden deck that offered a nice view of the marina. They served fried shrimp, crawfish, crab, gumbo, and other seafood dishes. There was plenty of cold beer and girls in skimpy shorts serving it.

We talked to the manager.

"Honestly, I don't recall seeing anything. I can ask around, but there's no way to track down the patrons that were here during that timeframe. Even if you could, our clientele likes to drink. Half of them can't remember their names by the time they leave."

I thanked him for his time and stepped onto the patio deck and surveyed the Marina. The office was obstructed here and there by the yachts and sailboats. It would have been easy for someone to force Kingston onto a boat without drawing much attention. Between the loud music and the raucous clientele, you could probably shoot someone in the marina, and the bar goers wouldn't notice.

JD got a text from Belinda. "She wants to meet up for happy hour."

"She must really be into you?" I said.

"I guess so. The girl's going to be the death of me. I don't know if I can keep up. But I'm damn sure going to try," he said with a twinkle in his eyes.

He dropped me off at *Diver Down*. I pretty much figured I wouldn't hear from him for the rest the evening.

I strolled back to the *Slick'n Salty* and took a nap. Sleeping on the couch had left my back angry, and I didn't exactly sleep well. I figured I'd go to Scarpetti's standing poker game that he had on Friday nights. It was a $10,000 buy-in. The last time I played, I got lucky and walked with a considerable amount of cash—most of which I still had stashed under my bunk. It was no secret that Scarpetti's game was a *Who's Who* of the area. Celebrities, gangsters, city officials— anybody who had the money to get into the game. And just like Vegas, what went on around the table, stayed around the table.

I showed up early, played a few hands and walked with $52,000. Not as much as I had won the last time, but not bad for less than an hour's work.

I was considering a career change.

Every Friday night, Scarpetti converted the luxury suite at the *Seven Seas* into a miniature casino. He had a bar stocked with top shelf liquor, and beautiful models to serve it. There were a selection of fine cigars, kept in a state-of-the-art humidor. I hung out at the bar and sipped a glass of whiskey. I knew Scarpetti would come talk to me sooner or later.

"I see you're on another winning streak," the gangster said.

"Just lucky, I guess."

"I'm telling you, you should come to my *big* game. $100,000 buy-in."

"Maybe."

"A guy like you would do well there. You've got the stones for it. There's ice water in your veins, no doubt about it."

"It's only money."

Scarpetti chuckled. "Only money. I like that."

"Speaking of money, did you hear Scott Kingston got killed?"

The gangster's smile faded. "A damn shame. I liked that guy. Good parties. Owed me a lot of money." He paused, his suspicious eyes surveying me. "Why do you mention it?"

"I figure a man like you would want to know who did the hit. After all, whoever killed Kingston took money out of your pocket, did they not?"

I had his full attention.

"What's your angle?"

"I just want to find out who did it, and something tells me you do too."

He paused for a long moment, pondering whether he wanted to have this conversation. "Who are you?"

"I'm just a guy who solves problems."

There was another long, uncomfortable pause.

"Step into my office," Scarpetti finally said.

He motioned to the next room.

I stepped into the private room with trepidation.

Two bodyguards, with 9mms strapped in shoulder holsters, followed. The door closed behind us, and once again I found myself in a room with an influential Mafia boss—and I wasn't exactly sure what my odds were of leaving the room still breathing.

"Word on the street is that Carlos Dominguez was upset with Kingston," Scarpetti said.

"Just released from Raiford?"

"Yeah. I can't prove this, you understand. And even if I could, my hands are tied."

"How so?"

"Dominguez is a member of *Rey Rojo*. My people don't want to go to war. So right now, the guy gets a free pass."

"Why tell me?"

"Because you are a problem solver. It's no secret you're working with Sheriff Daniels."

He noticed the surprise on my face.

"Not much happens on this island that I don't know about. So, if you happen to bust Carlos, and he goes back to prison, I'll feel a tiny bit of satisfaction."

11

"Tyson," a shaky voice filtered through my phone. "I need you to come get me."

"Scarlett, what's going on?" I answered, my brow tense with concern.

"You're not with Jack, are you?"

"No. I'm just about to leave a poker game. Is everything okay?"

"No," she cried.

I could barely hear over the thumping music in the background. "Where are you?"

"I'm at *Bumper*. Hurry!"

"I'll be there in a few."

"I'm in the back, in a booth."

She hung up the phone, and I stormed out of the hotel room. I caught a cab over to *Bumper* on Oyster Avenue. It was a trendy dance club that thumped techno music into the wee hours of the morning. There was a line around the block—girls in black cocktail dresses and stiletto heels, faces painted with sultry makeup. Guys dressed in starched shirts and over-styled hair. It wasn't quite Studio 54, but it wasn't exactly easy to get into.

I flashed my badge and bypassed the line—*and the exorbitant cover charge*. Inside the club, the music was deafening. Colored lights swirled, and fog hazed the dance floor as the rich and beautiful crowd undulated in a rhythmic motion.

I plowed through the horde, my head on a swivel, searching for Scarlett. She sounded terrified on the phone, and her speech had a slight slur to it. I figured she probably had too much to drink and got into a fight with her boyfriend.

I didn't see her anywhere.

She wasn't in the booth by the back bar where she said she would be. I made a few laps around the club with no success. I asked the bartender at the back bar if he'd seen a girl that fit Scarlett's description, but he was no help.

The girl standing next to me said, "There is a girl passed out in the bathroom."

I darted down the dim hallway that led to the restrooms. I burst through the door and flashed my badge and shouted, "Deputy Sheriff!"

I was met with awkward stares, but that was about it. I found Scarlett passed out on the floor in the corner. Nobody bothered to help her. They acted like she wasn't there.

I knelt down beside her and nudged her awake. Her eyes peeled open for a moment. A faint glimmer of recognition flickered in them before she closed them again. Her eyes were dilated and looked like black saucers.

"What did you take?"

"I don't know," she slurred.

I scooped her in my arms and carried her out of the restroom and stormed through the club.

Scarlett faded in and out of consciousness.

I called 911, and the flashing lights from the ambulance illuminated the sidewalk a few minutes later.

"Do you know what she took?" the EMT asked.

I shook my head.

They loaded her on a gurney and lifted her into the back of the ambulance. One of the paramedics started an IV while the other took her vital signs.

Her pulse and respiration were low.

The EMT shined a flashlight into her eyes checking for pupillary response. He administered an anti-opioid, Naloxone. The drug had a high binding affinity for the opioid receptors. It reversed the effect of opioids, and within two minutes of the injection, Scarlett came out of her overdosed state. Her respiration returned to normal about the time we arrived at the ER.

She was triaged and admitted to the ER, and I waited with her in the room while they did blood work and monitored her situation.

"Am I in trouble?" Scarlett asked.

"I'd say you're in a lot of trouble."

"I mean, like I'm not going to get arrested, am I?"

"No. They don't arrest people when they overdose."

"But, is this going to go down on my record, or something?"

"It will be noted in your medical history, but that's not going to go to law enforcement."

"Are you gonna tell my dad?" she asked, cringing.

"I think that's the least of your worries, right now," I said. "What the hell were you doing?"

"I was just trying to have a good time."

"Well, you succeeded," I said, my voice dripping with sarcasm.

Her eyes narrowed at me.

"You are in no position to give me dirty looks. What did you take?"

"I don't know. Obviously not what I thought I was taking."

"Where did you get it from?"

She didn't say anything.

"Scarlett...?"

"Okay, fine. Justin gave me some Molly. At least, I thought it was Molly. Then I started to feel really weird. Like not normal. That's when I called you."

"What happened to Justin?"

"I don't know. He said he was coming right back, and I guess he just took off."

I clenched my teeth. I could understand JD's frustration with the guy—and he had no idea this was going on.

"You can't tell Jack. He'll never let me see Justin again."

"Why would you want to?"

She shrugged. "I don't know," she said in a sad, pathetic voice.

"How long have you been doing this stuff?"

"What's the big deal? It's just Molly."

"It's not Molly. You realize you almost died?"

"Please don't be mad at me."

I tried to contain my frustration. "I'm not mad at you. I am concerned."

A doctor pushed into the room with a grim look on his face. He was a young guy with dark hair, teal scrubs, and a white lab coat with a stethoscope around his neck. *Dr. Patel* was embroidered on his lab coat and several identification badges were clipped onto his breast pocket. "You are very lucky to be alive, young lady. We found traces of meth-amphetamine, an unknown designer drug, and a lethal amount of Fentanyl." He glanced to me. "You got to her just in time."

My eyes widened, and I exchanged a glance with Scarlett. She needed to understand how close she came.

"What is your relationship to the patient?"

"Friend of the family," I said.

"Vital signs look good. We'd like to keep her overnight, just to make sure everything's okay. We also want to make sure you don't go into withdrawals. Are you a regular opioid user?"

Scarlett's face twisted. "No. I'm not a junkie!"

"I hope you will consider this a wake up call and be much more careful about what you put into your body," Dr. Patel said. "I don't want to see you back here, or worse, I don't want to read about you in the obituary section."

"I promise. That's the last time I take any drugs," Scarlett said.

"For your sake, I hope so."

12

"As I said, I'd like to admit you to the hospital and keep you overnight," Dr. Patel said. "We'll do a patient evaluation and have you consult with an addiction counselor."

"I am not an addict," Scarlett said. "It was an accident. I didn't know it was an opioid. I'm fine. I just want to go home."

"Are you refusing treatment?"

"I'm telling you, I'm fine. I didn't OD on purpose. I'm not suicidal. I'm not a drug addict. I just want to go home."

"Scarlett, I think it would be a good idea if you stayed," I said.

"No!"

"Alright," Patel said with a frustrated voice. "I can't force you to stay. I'll note in your file that you're declining further treatment and you're leaving against medical advice. I'll have your discharge papers ready shortly."

It took another two hours to push all the paperwork through the system.

"Can you pay for this, and I'll pay you back?" Scarlett asked.

"Don't you have insurance?"

"Yeah, I'm on Jack's policy. But I don't want him to get a bill. Please?" She asked, making a pouty face, looking at me with those adorable, sad eyes.

This girl knew how to get everything she wanted from a man.

"I haven't decided whether I'm going to tell your father."

"I swear. I will be on my best behavior from now on. No more hard partying. No more recreational drugs." She paused. "Except weed. Weed is still cool, right?"

I thought about it for a long moment, then sighed. "I'll keep your little secret. But there are a few conditions..."

"Anything."

"You pay me back every penny. You cut this shit out right now, and if I even think you're doing something you shouldn't, I'm telling Jack, and you're going straight to rehab."

"Deal." She grabbed my arm and smiled. In a soft voice, she said. "Thank you, Tyson."

"You owe me, big time."

Once we got her discharge papers, we stopped at the administration desk. I had fat stacks of cash stuffed in my pockets from my poker winnings. The hospital administrator's eyes bulged when I pulled out the wad and peeled off four crisp $100 bills.

Emergency room visits aren't cheap.

"Jesus Christ, Tyson! What did you do, rob a bank?" Scarlett asked.

"The cards fell my way tonight."

"Shit, teach me how to play poker."

"I will if it will keep you out of trouble."

"You make one mistake, and you're branded for life," she said, sighing dramatically for effect.

"Newsflash. You've screwed up more than once."

She gasped, feigning offence. "Okay, last time was not my fault."

"If you would have left town like you were supposed to, you wouldn't have been kidnapped."

"When you were my age, did you always listen to your parents?"

"Yes, I was a model child," I lied.

Scarlett rolled her eyes. "I'm hungry. Let's get something to eat."

We caught a cab over to *Drifter's Diner*. The late-night crowd was already starting to straggle in. The hostess seated us in a booth in the back, and we perused the laminated menus.

Scarlett ordered a cheeseburger, fries, and a chocolate shake. I ordered the same, minus the shake.

"Are you sure you're going to be able to keep that down?" I asked.

"All I know is that I've got a hole in my stomach. Greasy fast food always seems to settle my stomach."

"How are you feeling?"

"Like I got hit by a freight train, but I'll survive," she said.

"So, what's with you and this Justin guy? Are you dating him just to irritate your dad?"

"Is it working?" A thin grin tugged at her lips.

"If that's your goal, I'd say it's been pretty effective."

"I'm not trying to irritate anybody. I like Justin. But, it kind of was a dick move to abandon me."

"You think?"

A few text messages dinged her phone. Scarlett chuckled when she looked at the screen. "Speak of the devil."

She showed me the display.

"Fuck him," she grumbled. "I'm not texting him back."

"Well, at least you've made one smart decision tonight."

"How long are you going to harass me for this?"

"For as long as I can."

"Keep it up, and you're gonna lose your status as my favorite person."

"I'm your favorite person?" I asked, incredulous.

She smiled. "Yeah. You're cool, laid-back, and always getting me out of tight spots."

I gave her a skeptical glance. "I'm not loaning you any money, if that's why you're buttering me up."

She gasped again. "It was a genuine compliment!" Then she added, "But you are paying for dinner."

"I figured as much."

The waitress clanked down our plates, and we dug into our meal. Scarlett scarfed the burger down like she hadn't eaten in a month. She didn't seem any worse for the wear.

The resilience of youth.

We finished our meal, and I paid the tab and left a healthy tip. Scarlett's phone dinged with another text. "Looks like Dad is getting lucky tonight. He says he's not coming home."

She showed me the display.

"Can I stay at your place tonight?" she asked, innocently.

"Absolutely not!"

"Didn't the doctor say I shouldn't be left unsupervised tonight?"

I cringed. "He said you should be admitted to the *hospital* so you can be supervised. I can call JD and tell him your situation. I'm sure he'd be happy to come home and babysit you."

She snarled at me. "I can stay in the guest stateroom. I won't cause any trouble. I'll be gone before you wake up in the morning." She paused, trying to think of something to sweeten the pot with. "I'll even cook you breakfast in the morning, if you want."

My face crinkled with indecision. This was a bad idea, but the last thing she needed was to be left alone.

"Come on," she pleaded. "What if I need medical attention during the night?"

"No shenanigans. And you're out at sunrise."

Her pearly teeth sparkled as she smiled bright. "Yay, sleepover!"

I shook my head.

This was definitely going to be a mistake.

We caught a cab back to *Diver Down*. The parking lot was empty, and Madison had already closed the bar for the evening.

We strolled down the dock and climbed the transom to the *Slick'n Salty*. I unlocked the hatch and let Scarlett into the salon. "You know where everything is. Make yourself at home. Guest quarters are there, and you've got a private head."

"I know my way around this boat," she reminded me.

"Oh, and no visitors."

She rolled her eyes. "Do I look like I want to entertain visitors? I'm going to take a shower. I feel gross. Do you have towels?"

"There's one in there," I said. "I'll look in on you during the night, make sure you're okay."

She smiled and kissed me on the cheek. "Thanks, Tyson. I really appreciate this."

I went into my stateroom and locked the hatch behind me. I stuffed my winnings with my other cash, got undressed, and climbed into bed.

13

I woke up the next morning to the smell of bacon. I crawled out of bed, slipped on some shorts, and pushed into the salon.

Scarlett was doing something you should never do—cook bacon naked.

I covered my eyes and tried not to look, but that initial glance was already etched on my retinas. "Would you put some clothes on?"

"Please, it's not like you've never seen a pair of tits before."

"Not yours."

"I'm quite fond of them. What do you think?" She demonstrated her gravity defying properties by extending her chest and bouncing slightly.

I kept my eyes covered. "I think you need to get dressed now."

She huffed. "You're no fun."

She sauntered past me, brushing against me on purpose before she slipped into the guest stateroom.

I swallowed hard, and my cheeks must have been a brilliant shade of red. I took a deep breath and tried to regain my composure, then stepped into the galley and took over breakfast.

Scarlett emerged a few moments later with her skimpy black dress on from the night before, holding her pumps in her hand. "Do you have a scrunchie or something I can pull my hair back with?"

"I'm fresh out of beauty supplies.."

She made a pouty face.

I dished up our breakfast—bacon, eggs, toast, hashbrowns, and orange juice—and we took a seat in the lounge.

"How are you feeling?" I asked.

"Not too bad, surprisingly. I mean, considering I almost died. Do you have any ibuprofen?"

"Yeah." I moved back to the galley, and pulled a bottle from a storage compartment and tossed it to her. It rattled like a shaker when she caught it. Scarlett popped the top and swallowed three gel caps with a gulp of orange juice.

"You swear you're not going to tell Dad?"

"I'm not going to lie to him if he asks. But if he doesn't ask, we can pretend it didn't happen—as long as you don't do something stupid like this again."

"My stupid days are over. Promise." She held up her hand like a scout.

Her promises were about as good as a banknote in Venezuela.

I took a seat back at the table and Scarlett shoveled down her breakfast. When she was done, she checked her phone and her social media accounts. "What a jackass. I am so not talking to him anymore."

"Justin? I think that's a good idea."

"Look at this." She showed me her phone. "I got 30 texts from him last night."

"Don't answer."

"I'm not going to. I'm so pissed off at him."

I finished my eggs, and Scarlett took both our plates to the galley and washed them. "So, what are we doing today?"

"We?"

"I meant that in the general sense, as in *what are you doing today?*"

"You are going home. I'd have a hell of a lot of explaining to do if Jack caught you here."

"Aw, you're not afraid of my dad, are you?" she said in a saucy tone.

"I don't think you want him getting a full explanation of last night's events, do you?"

Her sassy smile faded. "I'm gone."

Scarlett strutted out of the galley, grabbed her heels and gave me a hug goodbye. "Thanks for saving my life."

She lifted on her tiptoes and kissed my cheek."

Somebody turned up the heat. It felt hot and stuffy in the salon all of a sudden. My body tensed, and I swallowed hard.

"It's so much fun making you squirm." She whirled around and sauntered to the aft hatch. Before leaving, she called back into the salon, "Stay out of trouble."

I chuckled, and breathed a sigh of relief when she was gone.

A few minutes later, an enraged Madison called. "Did I just see what I *think* I saw?"

"It's not what it looks like."

"Really? So, you want to tell me why Scarlett was leaving your boat this morning, doing the walk of shame?"

"Nothing happened."

"Yeah, right. You expect me to believe a hot 18-year-old stayed at your place and you didn't bang her?"

"She got in a little bit of trouble last night, and I helped her out. That's it."

"I'll bet you helped her. And just when I was starting to think you might be a decent guy. You better hope JD doesn't find out."

"Madison—"

She hung up.

No good deed goes unpunished.

I should have listened to the little voice in the back of my head that said this was going to cause way too much drama.

Not five minutes later, JD called.

I let it ring a few times before answering the phone. I don't know exactly what I was expecting. I thought that perhaps Madison had ratted me out, and I would have some explaining to do. My voice shook with nerves, but I put on a bright smile. "Hey, what's going on?"

"We are in business?"

"What do you mean?"

"Ashley hacked Kingston's computer. She hit the mother lode."

"Surveillance footage?"

"Yup. And it tells us everything we need to know. I'll swing by your place in a few."

14

I watched a video on JD's phone. He had downloaded it from Ashley. She still had Scott's computer and was working on some other encrypted files, but she had managed to unlock all the security footage from Kingston's marina. The footage showed Kingston and an unidentified man getting onto a Go-Fast boat on the evening of his disappearance and leaving the harbor. Ashley said she scanned through the later footage and never saw any evidence of the boat returning.

"Can we get a screen grab and run a facial recognition check?"

"Done. That's Carlos Dominguez. Ashley got a match in the facial recognition database."

"Looks like he's our guy," I speculated.

"Do you want to do a *knock and talk?*" JD asked. "Or should we see if we can get a warrant?"

"You mean you don't just want to raid the place?" I asked, full of sarcasm.

"I do, but I figured you'd want to play by the rules."

"Let's take it to Daniels and let him put it before a judge."

"That's what I figured you'd say. I'll get on it." He paused a moment. "What did you do last night?"

I hesitated. "Nothing."

"I'm telling you. Belinda has some hot friends. You need to get back on the horse."

"I'm staying off the horse for a little while."

"Are you sure about that?" JD asked, as he spotted a pair of black panties on the deck. He walked across the compartment and scooped the frilly things off the floor.

I nearly had a heart attack.

"Staying off the horse, are you?" he said in disbelief.

I was at a loss for words. My face went pale. I stammered, "I don't know how those got there."

"I sure as hell do."

I hoped to God he didn't.

"Come on, spill the beans."

This was about the time I began to wonder if he knew more than he was letting on. I hadn't done anything wrong. But I felt guilty as hell. Maybe because it took all of my willpower to ignore the temptation.

"Those must be Aria's. She must have left those behind," I said.

I felt like he could totally see through my bullshit. I was a damn good liar—it was a requirement in my line of work—but I felt like the worst liar in the world at the moment.

He tossed them back on the deck.

"I'm meeting Belinda and her friends over at the *Crazy Conch* tonight. You should come along. She's got this little redheaded friend—emerald eyes, creamy skin, and a body that will make you want to climb right back on that horse. 22, smart, funny. She's right up your alley."

"I'll consider it."

"Because if you don't get on that. I'm gonna have to work a three-some between Belinda and this girl."

"Well, I wouldn't want to get in the way of that."

"I know you're bummed about Aria. I can see it on your face. I just don't want my buddy sulking around like a loser."

My face crinkled. "I am not a loser."

"Of course you're not a loser," he said patronizingly. "You got dumped by a hot model. It happens to the best of us."

"I didn't get dumped."

"Yeah, you did," JD said. "Look, all I'm saying is you can't stay on the sidelines for too long. It will screw with your head. You'll grow cobwebs on that thing and you'll get performance anxiety. Next thing you know, you're popping little blue pills just to get the job done."

"Speak for yourself. I don't have to pop little blue pills."

"No need to get hostile."

"Don't you have somewhere to be?" I asked, perturbed.

"Actually, I do. I'm meeting Belinda for lunch."

"Again? You sure are starting to spend a lot of time with that girl."

"She's going back to *The World* in a few days. I'm trying to make every moment count."

"So this is just one of those Coconut Key things?"

"Thank God for Coconut Key things." He headed for the hatch. "I'll talk to Daniels. But since it's the weekend, we probably won't get any movement on this until Monday. But that doesn't mean we can't do a little recce on our target."

Jack left, and I breathed another sigh of relief as I sat on the lounge. I stayed there for a few minutes, then strolled down the dock to *Diver Down*. I figured I needed a face to face with Madison. She busied herself behind the bar and didn't want to talk to me.

"I'm telling you, you've got the wrong idea."

"Don't try to talk your way out of this," Madison said.

"I'm not trying to talk my way out of anything. You've made an assumption based on incomplete facts."

"Well, the facts are pretty self-explanatory," she snapped. "But hey, it's your life. Live it how you choose. But don't be surprised when nobody shows up to your funeral."

I grimaced. That was pretty harsh. My natural response would have been to say that I wasn't planning on dying anytime soon. But in light of recent events—and having already died once—I was almost afraid to buy green bananas.

I could have told Madison the details of Scarlett's overdose, but I had promised to keep my mouth shut. Not that Madison was a gossiper, but it would probably find its way back to Jack eventually.

By the time I got back to the boat, Agent Archer was waiting for me.

15

"U h, oh," I said. "Am I in trouble?"

Archer laughed. Her smile was infectious. "Not yet. Actually, I came here to apologize."

"For what?"

"Being such a lightweight. Sorry you had to witness that."

"It was amusing."

"For you," she said. "Anyway, thank you for looking after me."

"Not a problem."

"Let me buy you lunch in an effort to make it up to you."

I scoffed. "You think you're going to get off the hook that easy?"

Her eyes widened. "Looks like I'm the one who's in trouble now."

"I've got a free afternoon. I was thinking about going for a dive. I could use a buddy. Do you have your advanced diver certification?"

"I do."

"Good. It's settled."

She looked at me with suspicious eyes. "Are you just trying to get me into a bikini?"

"I've already seen you in your underwear."

Her cheeks flushed." Right. Don't remind me."

"It wasn't half bad."

She arched an eyebrow.

"I mean, from what I could see. I'd have to get a better look before I could really comment."

"A better look, eh?" Archer eyed me curiously. "Let me think about it over lunch."

"I've got the tanks charged and the gear is all prepped."

"Okay. Fine," she conceded. "I usually don't dive with people I don't know well. But despite outward appearances, I think you're pretty squared away."

I feigned offense. "Despite outward appearances?"

"Yeah, I'm going to have to reserve judgment until I get to know you better."

I laughed. "Are you comfortable with a deep dive?"

"How deep?"

"110 feet?"

"We don't know each other well enough."

"Good answer. When was the last time you were that deep?"

"Maybe two months ago?"

"Like anything else, skills degrade over time."

"I'm in prime form," she said.

"I've seen."

Her eyes narrowed at me.

"How about we do something easy like Pelican Reef? 30 feet."

We grabbed lunch at Tsunami Jacks, then swung by her place. She put on a skimpy blue spaghetti string bikini, which was a treat for the eyes. She grabbed her tank and gear and we headed back to the marina. We boarded the *Slick'n Salty* and headed out to sea.

It was a beautiful day—clear skies, warm sun, and a gentle breeze. I brought the boat on plane, and the engines rumbled as we raced across the water. It was amazing how quickly the rest of the world faded away when you were on the water. Nothing else mattered. All your troubles and worries would melt away with the amber sun.

We arrived at the dive site within an hour. I attached to a mooring buoy and flew a dive flag. The red and white fabric flickered with the breeze. I checked the gear again making sure the tanks were full, gauges were working correctly, and the regulators functioned.

I helped Archer with her tank, and a few moments later we plunged into the water.

The temperature was perfect, and the teal water was crystal clear. Once we were at depth, we were treated to a visual feast. An array of colorful fish darted about the reef. We saw Queen Angelfish, edged with blue accents and yellow bodies. Spotted Butterfly fish flitted about the coral. I saw polkadotted Yellowtail Damselfish. A Banded Jawfish hovered in a crevice, looking like some type of sea monster. There were an endless assortment of these magnificent ocean dwellers. With nothing but the sound of the regulator and the burble of bubbles, the reef was like a meditation chamber.

Until something went wrong.

Bubbles rocketed from Archer's regulator, and the hose flailed about like an angry snake. Archer's eyes filled with panic. Sometimes cold water dives can cause the regulator to freeze up from internal condensation, but we were practically diving in bathwater.

I finned to Archer and handed her my alternate regulator. She placed it into her mouth and sucked a breath of air. I motioned for her to stay calm and breathe normally. We slowly ascended and made a safety stop. I still had plenty of air left for the two of us.

We finally broke through the surface, and Archer took a breath. "I don't know what happened. I just had everything serviced, and the gear looked fine on my pre-dive check."

"It's a good thing we didn't do that deep dive," I said.

We swam to the boat, and I helped Archer climb over the transom. We slipped our tanks off, and I inspected her regulator. In the back of my mind I couldn't help but wonder if her equipment had been tampered with? I knew Isabella wanted her out of the way.

"What's the matter?" she said. The distressed look on my face must have given me away.

"Nothing," I said. "Sometimes these things happen."

She had kept her composure, but I could tell she was a tad unsettled. The *what if* scenarios can often be more traumatic than the actual event. This could have gone so many shades of wrong had we been at a deeper depth.

"That's twice you saved me," she said. "I promise, I'm not always this much of a problem child."

"Well, despite outward appearances..."

"Shut up," she said, playfully.

"I can't take you anywhere. Not to a bar. Not to a reef..."

"I was trying to redeem myself, but it seems I just keep digging a bigger hole. Maybe I should avoid you?"

"You'd miss me."

Her eyes narrowed at me. "Your modesty is your most impressive quality," she said, her voice full of sarcasm.

"Actually, that's not my most impressive quality."

She blushed at my insinuation. "Okay, well, so," she fumbled for something else to talk about, "how about those Bucs?"

"It's the off season."

"Right..." she cleared her throat. Well, if you'll excuse me, I'm going to use the little girl's room. She sauntered into the salon and found the head.

I noticed a *Go-Fast* boat approaching. It sped across the water, leaving a wake of white water in its trail. The engine roared like a race-car.

I didn't think much of it, until it pulled alongside the *Slick'n Salty*. Two men, their faces obscured by race helmets, pulled out black submachine guns and opened fire.

16

Muzzle flash flickered from the barrels. The bullets snapped past me, whizzing through the air, peppering the fiberglass hull.

I dove to the deck and crawled toward the salon. My gun was inside.

Debris splintered everywhere—bits of fiberglass and fragments of the wood paneling.

I crawled across the deck on my belly. "Archer, stay down!"

I grabbed my gun from within my stateroom. Bullets tore through the salon, cracking windows, shattering my flatscreen TV. By the time I made it back to the aft hatch, the gunfire stopped.

Then the situation got worse.

The goons in the *Go-Fast* boat lobbed a fragmentation grenade onto the *Slick'n Salty*. It bounced across the deck, into the cockpit, tumbling toward me.

My eyes bulged, and I scampered toward the grenade. I scooped it up, hoping I'd have enough time to toss it overboard. There was a distinct possibility I was going to lose an appendage along with my head, and the rest of my body.

I hurled it through the air toward the *Go-Fast* boat just as they sped away. It plunged into the water and exploded a fraction of a second later. A plume of white water sprayed into the air like a geyser erupting.

I moved to the gunwale and angled my weapon over the ledge and opened fire at the *Go-Fast* boat as it sped away, spitting white water as it disappeared on the horizon.

I emptied my entire magazine for good measure.

I doubt I hit anything, but I was pissed off. It felt good to vent a little frustration. The sharp smell of gunpowder filled my nostrils, and the report of the weapon echoed across the water.

My heart pounded in my chest, and adrenaline rushed through my veins. I knew, in a few moments, the crash would come, now that the situation was diffused. I checked myself for injuries, then darted into the salon to check on Archer. "Are you okay?"

The hatch to the head pushed open and and Archer crawled out. Her face was pale and her eyes were round like saucers.

"Are you hit?" I asked.

"She shook her head. I don't think so."

Her hands trembled, and she looked frazzled.

"Your first firefight?" I asked.

She nodded.

"It gets easier."

"Does this kind of thing happen to you all the time?"

"Pretty much."

"Remind me never to go diving with you."

A grim chuckle escaped my lips. "I'm not sure I'm the one they were after."

Archer's brow crinkled. "Who would want to kill me?"

I shrugged. "I don't know you well enough to comment."

"Not funny."

"You are looking into some pretty heavy hitters. Maybe that was a message?"

My first thought was that Isabella had sent operatives to take out Agent Archer, figuring I wasn't going to do the job. But this wasn't Cobra Company's style. This was far too crude. Sabotaging a regulator? Definitely Cobra Company's style. A drive-by shooting? Not so much.

I pressed the mag release button and dropped the magazine from my pistol and slapped in another one. I pulled the slide back, charging a round into the chamber. I flicked the weapon on safe, then holstered it. I planned on keeping the weapon close by the rest of the day.

I checked the engine compartment, and the fuel lines, to make sure no critical structures had been damaged in the gunfight. Everything seemed okay, but there was a possibility I missed something.

Most of the damage was cosmetic. All of the nice cabinetry in the salon was splintered and pocked with bullet holes. The fiberglass hull looked like Swiss cheese.

Once I was sure there were no fuel lines ruptured, I cranked the engines up and headed us back toward the marina. I kept a pretty slow pace for the first several minutes, making sure everything operated properly.

Archer was still unsettled. She stayed in the salon for a while, then joined me on the bridge deck.

"You hanging in there?" I asked.

She nodded.

"Want a beer?"

"No. I think I want to keep my head clear."

She got on the phone and reported the incident to her agency. The attempted murder of a federal agent wasn't something that was treated lightly.

When we got back to the marina, we went down to the station and filed a report. The next day, FBI investigators would come down from DC, and there would be lots and lots of paperwork.

Archer was ready for that beer by the time we finished at the station.

17

"**I**'m sticking with beer, I promise," Archer said. "No more margaritas."

We had gone over to *Billy's Big Wave* for happy hour. Surf music filled the air, and long boards hung on the wall. There were pictures of famous surfers from the 60s through to the present day. It reminded me of the Hard Rock Café, but with surfing memorabilia.

Archer's nerves had begun to settle. But she still wasn't comfortable. The first beer took the edge off. The second brought her to baseline.

"So, you really grabbed a grenade and threw it back at them?"

"Yup."

"You don't seem freaked out at all."

"You can't let this stuff get to you. You don't want fear creeping around inside your head. We all have to die some-time. What matters is what you do with the time you've been given. And when the time comes, you greet death without fear."

"You should write self-help books. Sounds very stoic."

"*Memento Mori*," I said. "Embrace the fact that you going to die. Make this life count. We don't often get a second chance."

I'm guessing you've been close a number of times," she asked.

"Closer than you can possibly imagine."

"So, are you ever going to tell me your story? Or are you just going to keep me guessing?"

"I don't want to take the mystery out of our relationship," I said, coyly.

"So, this is a relationship?"

"Sure. We have a relationship... You get in trouble, I get you out."

She sneered at me playfully.

The waitress returned. "Can I get you another round.?"

"Absolutely," I said.

"No. Two is my limit."

"Don't be a party pooper."

She looked at me flatly. "Because I was loads of fun the other night..."

"True." I turned to the waitress. "She's cut off. But keep them coming for me."

Archer shot me a look. "I am not cut off. I am voluntarily choosing to moderate my consumption."

"Yeah, I'd rather you didn't pass out on me tonight." I said. "But you were kind of adorable when you were puking in the bathroom."

Her head fell into her hands, embarrassed. "Okay. What's it going to cost me to make that memory go away?"

"I'm sorry, I don't accept bribes. You just have to live with it."

"Are you sure there's nothing I can do to change your opinion of me?"

It was a loaded question.

"I could maybe think of a few things," I said with a mischievous grin.

"Could you, now?" she replied with a flirty twinkle in her eyes.

Near-death experiences and traumatic events affect people in different ways. It pushes some people deeper into their shell. Some grow extremely fearful and seek to minimize risk. For others, it does quite the opposite. It brings them out, and they desire to experience all that life has to offer, knowing it may end at any moment. I think it affected Agent Archer in the latter.

By the time we got back to the *Slick'n Salty,* our lips were practically glued together.

We tumbled into the salon, peeling each other's clothes off, leaving a trail behind us. She looked even better out of the swimsuit than she did in it.

We tumbled around in bed, and let me tell you, she acted like this was the last time she might ever get laid.

When it was all done, we collapsed beside each other in a state of post orgasmic bliss. She slinked her body around me and stroked my chest. "I'm sure that was another bad judgment call, but it was a lot of fun."

"Yes it was," I said.

We basked in the afterglow for a moment.

The sound of the aft hatch squeaking broke me out of my stupor. I lurched up, grabbed my pistol, and advanced to the hatch of my stateroom.

Jen sat up in bed, fumbling for her weapon.

I pushed into the salon and almost had a heart attack. The air escaped my lungs, and I froze for a moment.

I lowered my weapon. I was relieved that the boat hadn't been infiltrated by a team of assassins. But I had mixed feelings about seeing Aria, in light of the current situation.

She smiled cautiously. "Hi?"

"What did I tell you about sneaking up on me?"

"Sorry, I forgot. I was just so excited and I wanted to surprise you."

"What happened to New York?"

She made a pouty face. "I missed you."

She moved close, but she quickly sensed that something was wrong. "You don't look thrilled to see me."

"No. I am. It's just that..."

She peered around me and saw Agent Archer.

Her cheeks flushed. "Oh my God! I feel like such an idiot."

Her eyes brimmed, and she spun around and marched toward the hatch.

I chased after her and grabbed her arm. "Aria, wait. It's not what it seems."

She jerked her arm free. "You don't owe me any explanations," she said, trying to sound detached.

"Wait. Just let me explain."

Aria marched into the cockpit, hopped the transom, and strolled down the dock.

I continued after her. "You were the one who dumped me! Remember?"

She stopped in her tracks and turned around. "I didn't dump you."

There was a long pause between us.

"You kind of did."

She took a few steps closer to me. "I didn't know what to do. My life was on hold. And my career was going down the tubes. And I didn't want you to have this obligation to me. Once I got back to New York, I felt like I made a big mistake. So I came back here. And you've moved on. Rather quickly, I see."

"I haven't moved on. It—"

"You don't have to explain anything," she said, softly.

She was trying desperately to hold back tears, and failing. "I gotta go. I need some time. We'll talk later."

She turned around and stormed down the dock. By this time, Archer marched out of the salon.

I turned to face her and forced a smile. "You don't have to leave."

"Yes, I do. I need to salvage a little bit of my dignity." She strolled by and gave me a kiss on the cheek. "It was fun, Tyson. Poor judgment on my part, but fun."

She spun around and marched toward *Diver Down*.

I let out a frustrated breath and clenched my fists and growled at the sky.

What lousy timing!

18

"Sounds like you got on the horse, and got thrown right back off," JD said, his voice crackling through the speaker on my cell phone.

"Something like that." I replied.

I had told him about the previous nights drama with Aria and Agent Archer. I had tossed and turned most of the night and didn't get much sleep. It was 9am the next morning, and I was still lying in bed pondering how I was going to untangle the mess.

"I don't know what I'm going to do. I've been calling Aria, but she won't answer. I don't know where she's staying. It's an absolute cluster fuck."

"When I said get back on the horse, I didn't mean you should bang the FBI agent."

"Things happen."

"Well, pull yourself together. The judge signed off on a warrant to raid Carlos's place."

"Who's in on the raid?"

"Sheriff Daniels. SWAT. Unless you want to bring your FBI agent in on this?"

"No."

"Didn't think so."

"Let's go by the station, grab some vests, then take down this perp. It'll be just like old times."

"Do we know where he's at?"

"He's been living with his girlfriend since his release."

JD hung up, and was at the marina within 20 minutes. He freaked the fuck out when he saw his boat. It was the first time he had seen it since the incident. His eyes widened, and he looked like he was going to have a seizure. His face twitched uncontrollably. "What the hell happened? You said a few bullet holes."

I shrugged dismissively. "What? That is a *few* bullet holes."

"A few hundred!" he exclaimed, incredulous.

"It could have been a lot worse. You're lucky the damn thing didn't sink."

He glared at me.

"Hey, I'm not happy about this either. I live here, remember?"

"You know how much that's going to cost to fix?"

"You've got insurance, don't you?"

"That's beside the point."

"How long do you think it will take to fix?" I asked.

JD shrugged.

"It's going to put me out on the street for a little bit," I said, sounding pathetic.

JD's eyes narrowed at me. "I don't know if I want you staying at my place. My house might end up looking like this."

"Fine. I'm sure I can find someplace else to stay," I said, moping.

JD grumbled to himself and shook his head. "Come on. Let's get out of here. We've got work to do."

We geared up at the station and headed to the location with the SWAT team. Carlos's girlfriend had a small house on the west side of the island. According to her file, she'd been popped once on a small possession charge. She wasn't currently employed. It was my guess that she'd been living off cash that Carlos had stashed somewhere before his arrest. The house was in her name, but there was no doubt that Carlos paid for it.

We sat in the SWAT Tactical Response Van parked down the street from the target's house. I was already starting to sweat with the heavy bullet-proof vest on. I press checked my weapon and slipped an earbud into my ear canal so I could communicate with JD and the team.

Two SWAT officers advanced down the street, doing an initial recce of the house. They took infrared images of the house, and the live feed was pumped into the tactical vehicle, displayed on large-screen monitors. I watched several orange-red figures move about the house. Cooler colors were represented by blue.

"Looks like we've got three occupants total," an officer said, his voice crackling in my ear.

"Are we sure Carlos is in there?" Sheriff Daniels asked.

"Reasonably confident, sir," an officer responded.

Sheriff Daniels gave the nod, and we slipped out of the van and approached the house. The midday sun beat down hard. I advanced forward with the team, my weapon drawn, keeping it in a low ready position.

As we reached the property, the team split up, with several officers moving around to the rear. They all wore black tactical outfits with vests, helmets, and carried semiautomatic rifles.

JD and I took a position in front of the house, flattening our backs against the wall beside the door.

"I've got eyes on the target," a voice crackled in my earbud. "Two men and a woman."

"Are they armed?" Sheriff Daniels asked.

"Affirmative. I have a visual on a pistol holstered on the target's waist. There are what appear to be several kilos of cocaine on the table.

"This should be fun," JD muttered.

"Give me a signal when you're in position," Sheriff Daniels said

"Roger that. We are good to go."

Daniels looked around at the team, then banged on the door. He yelled, "Sheriff's Department. We have a warrant. Sheriff's Department! We have a warrant!"

There was some commotion inside.

Daniels nodded to officers holding a battering ram. They advanced forward, ready to slam the end of the heavy metal ram into the door.

The door exploded, showering splinters of wood in all directions as a shotgun blast shredded the door.

We all took cover.

Looks like the occupants didn't want any unwelcome visitors.

The SWAT team broke glass, scattering razor-sharp shards. They tossed in flash-bang grenades that exploded with a blinding flash, then filled the home with smoke.

There was shouting and an eruption of gunfire as the team stormed the house. We breached the front door, leapfrogging our way inside, clearing the area as we went.

The crackle of gunfire filled my ears. There were a few loud booms from the shotgun. Bits of sheet rock and gypsum exploded from the walls. My nostrils filled with the sharp smell of gunpowder. Muzzle flash flickered through the thick haze.

It was pure chaos.

Carlos's girlfriend didn't get too many shots off with the shotgun. The SWAT team peppered her full of bullets, her body jerking and twitching with each hit. Blood sprayed into the air, and she fell back to the tile. The shotgun clattered away as her sucking chest wound gurgled.

Several kilos of cocaine were stacked atop a table in the living room—Carlos had apparently resumed operations.

He retreated down the hallway and ducked into a bedroom. He angled his weapon around the doorframe and squeezed off a few rounds. The muzzle flash illuminated the corridor.

Bullets snapped in all directions.

Smoke filled the hallway.

An officer fired several rounds into the sheetrock by the door Carlos hid behind.

A few seconds later, Carlos slumped to the ground, and his pistol tumbled from his hand, sliding into the hallway. The bullets had blasted through the gypsum and into Carlos's thoracic cavity. Blood flowed from the wounds.

The tactical squad advanced, clearing the area. One of them yelled, "Target acquired," as he reached Carlos's body.

Carlos twitched and convulsed as the last breath escaped his lungs.

I cringed, knowing we would never get any answers about why he killed Kingston.

If he killed Kingston.

I advanced down the corridor, and angled my weapon into another bedroom. There was a wide-eyed man in the corner with his hands up, displaying a badge. He had shaggy hair and a scruffy beard and looked like a beach bum. "FBI. Don't shoot."

19

"What the fuck is wrong with you people?" the shaggy haired FBI agent snarled. He looked like a rabid dog, frothing at the mouth. The veins bulged in his neck.

We were back at the station in a debriefing room. We gathered with Sheriff Daniels, along with the SWAT team. This was supposed to be a victory celebration. Instead it turned into a tongue lashing.

"We were just doing our job," Sheriff Daniels protested.

"Did you ever think to confer with the FBI on this?"

"I'm sorry, I didn't realize I had to ask your permission for every suspect we arrest," Daniels snarked.

"I've been working undercover for six months, trying to work my way up the food chain. Carlos just got out of prison, and he was hungry to get back in the game and prove himself a good earner for the *Rey Rojo* cartel. This was the second buy I had made from him in the last two weeks, and I was getting closer to an introduction to the higher ups. Now that's never going to happen."

Agent Archer stepped into the briefing room. We exchanged a glance that was full of tension. There were a lot of things to be discussed.

"Maybe you should have informed us of your operation?" Daniels said.

"We're pretty sure we have an internal problem," Archer said. "These cartels are getting assistance from the inside. We couldn't take the risk. This operation was strictly on a need to know basis."

"Then no one is at fault here. So take your bitching somewhere else," Daniels said, red in the face. "My men did a fantastic job today. And I will not have you coming in here and disparaging our work." He took a deep breath. "I think that concludes our debrief for the day."

He stormed out of the briefing room. The squad of tactical officers followed. JD flashed me a wary glance, anticipating some heated discussions between Archer and me.

"You two jackasses stay out of my way," the shaggy FBI agent grumbled as he stomped out of the room.

Archer followed.

I pushed away from the table and chased her into the hallway. "Agent Archer, do you have a minute?"

She stopped reluctantly, spun around, folded her arms, and sighed. "Yes, Deputy?"

"In private."

We stepped back into the briefing room, and JD waited in the hallway. I closed the door behind us. There was a long moment of silence.

"I understand why you didn't say anything about your sting," I said. "Operational security and all. I get it."

"There certainly were a lot of things that you failed to tell me," she said, snidely.

"I didn't know we were going to raid Carlos's place until this morning."

There was a long uncomfortable pause.

"You didn't tell me you had a girlfriend either."

"I don't have a girlfriend."

"So, she was just a crazy stalker that showed up out of nowhere?"

"We broke up. I didn't know she was coming back into town."

"Whatever. It's none of my business,"she said, trying to act dispassionate, but failing. She changed the subject again. "I guess you can chalk today up as a win."

"Not really. I still don't have definitive proof of who killed Kingston. But there is one less scumbag on the street."

"Is that all? Can I go now?" she asked in a sassy tone.

"What else are you not telling me?" I asked.

"Hmm, let's see. Oh, yeah... nothing."

My eyes narrowed at her.

"What? I don't have a boyfriend. Everything I've told you has been the truth. Except maybe the part that you were great in bed. I didn't want to hurt your feelings."

She gave me a sympathy pat on the way toward the door.

"You're a terrible liar," I said.

"Don't flatter yourself," she said as she grabbed the door handle.

"What's your connection to Kingston?"

She paused, then turned around. She grimaced as she thought about it for moment. Then she came clean. "He was a CI."

"And you didn't think it was important to tell me that he was a Confidential Informant?"

"He would give us tips from time to time."

"Is that why Carlos came after him?"

She shrugged. "Who knows?"

Archer spun around and left the briefing room. The fruity smell of her shampoo lingered in my nostrils. I clenched my jaw in frustration.

JD snickered when I stepped back into the hallway.

I gave him the side-eye. "So, what's next?"

"Happy hour is next. The perp is dead. We have no leads. This one goes unsolved. It will end up on one of those cold case TV shows in 20 years."

"Not acceptable," I said. "I'm not letting this one go."

"When have you ever let anything go?" JD muttered.

20

The sushi was half-price during happy hour at *Blowfish*. I'm usually always leery of discounted sushi, but *Blowfish* was the best on the island. It was an upscale joint. The stunning waitresses wore skintight bodysuits with low-cut necklines and fishnet leggings.

"Are you sure it's safe to eat here?" I asked.

I wasn't asking because I had concerns about the quality. The last time we were here, JD hooked up with one of the waitresses. Depending on how he left things, there was a possibility our food could be *contaminated*.

"Would you relax? There is no cause for alarm." Then he caught a glimpse of the waitress across the restaurant. "Oh shit. Keep your head down. It's Kaylee."

I grumbled under my breath. "She's going to spit on our food."

"Nonsense. We're sitting at the bar. We can see it from beginning to end."

Kaylee strolled past us and put a hand on JD's shoulder. "The 80s called. They want their hair back."

I tried not to spit out my beer as she sauntered away. "So, I'm guessing *that* ended well?"

Jack's eyes narrowed at me. "She's just being playful."

I didn't buy it for a minute.

We ordered the salmon, a spicy tuna roll, a California roll, a few pieces of eel, a couple of Kiran Lights, and a bottle of sake. Fortunately, JD's jilted lover didn't serve us. But I was pretty sure she had complained about him to all her waitress friends.

"How's Scarlett doing?" I asked.

"Don't quote me on it, but I think she dumped that Justin guy."

"Good."

"I don't know what's come over her lately, but she seems to be mellowing out a bit."

"Maybe she's maturing."

JD scoffed.

I felt bad about keeping a secret from him, but it seemed like there was no need to rehash the situation—as long as Scarlett was staying on the straight and narrow.

"Look, I'll make sure your boat gets back into *as new* condition," I said. "Don't worry about it. Whatever insurance doesn't pay for, I will."

"I appreciate that, buddy. I'm not worried about it. But it's nice that you offered."

Our meal was perfect. The fish tasted like it had been pulled out of the ocean this morning. Fresh and clean. The only other place where I'd had sushi this good was in Japan.

"I'm going to meet Belinda and her friends later. Do you want to come along?"

"I think I've got enough relationship drama at the moment." I pulled out my phone and texted Aria again, trying to get a response.

This time she replied:

[I'm back in New York. I'm not ignoring you. I just don't want to talk about it right now. No need to keep texting me.]

My brow lifted with surprise. I couldn't help but feel like I had been punched in the stomach. I showed the message to JD. "I guess she told me."

"Move on. There's nothing to see here. If it's meant to be, it'll be. If it's not, you'll find someone else in no time."

"Yeah, but I liked her."

"Well, you shouldn't have banged the FBI agent."

I scowled at him. "You were the one who told me to get back on the horse!"

"I didn't think you were actually stupid enough to listen to my advice. Look at me. You know how many ex-wives I've got. Whatever I say, you should probably do the opposite."

I glared at him and clenched my jaw.

JD's phone blew up with a bunch of texts. He slung the last gulp of beer down his throat. "I've got to run. Meeting Belinda and her friends at *Bumper*. Last chance?"

"That's all you."

"Text me if you change your mind." He motioned to the empty plates. "This one's on you, right?"

"Sure."

He surveyed the restaurant and darted out when Kaylee wasn't looking.

I finished the last few pieces of the spicy tuna roll, then flagged down our waitress. I was surprised at how cheap it was during happy hour. I left a wad of cash on the table, and strolled toward the door.

Kaylee stopped me before I could get to the hostess stand. She handed me her number. "Just because I know it will piss Jack off."

She winked at me and sauntered away.

I had no intention of ever using the number, but I was curious as to what Jack had done to get on her bad side.

I caught an Uber back to *Diver Down*, and stopped in for a drink at the bar. Madison gave me a dirty look. "Have you told Jack yet?"

"Told him what?"

"You know what." Her eyes burned into me.

"For the last time, I didn't sleep with her."

"You're going to break that girl's heart, and lose a best friend."

"Why aren't you listening to me?"

Her eyes narrowed at me. "You swear you didn't have sex with Scarlett?"

"I swear. I've got enough trouble as it is, I don't need to go adding that to my list."

Madison sighed, reluctantly. She was still skeptical. "What will it be?"

"I think I'll stick with beer for now."

She grabbed an ice cold bottle, popped the top, and slid it across the bar. It took me a moment to adjust to the taste after the Kiran Light.

I stayed for a few beers and watched the game. As I was leaving, the land-line phone rang. Madison answered behind the bar. Her face crinkled. "Yes, I'll accept."

Her quizzical expression changed to worry. "Scarlett, are you okay?"

I paused at the bar, my face tense with concern.

Madison's eyes flicked to mine. "Yeah, he's right here."

She handed the phone to me.

"Tyson?" Scarlett squeaked, her voice frail and timid.

"What's going on?"

"I need you to come get me out of here."

"Where is here?" I asked,

"I'm in jail. Dade County."

I lifted my brow, astonished. "What are you doing up there?"

"It's a long story."

"I'm listening," I said, waiting for an explanation. My mind raced with possibilities.

"It's not a big deal."

"Something tells me this is a big deal."

"Chloe and I were going to a club in South Beach. I don't want to talk about it on the phone."

"What are you being charged with?"

She hesitated. "Possession of a controlled substance. But it's not mine. I swear!"

My face scrunched up in anger. "You promised you weren't going to do this shit again!"

"Are you going to help me or not?" she cried.

I listened to her sob on the other end of the line. "I'm scared, Tyson. I really need your help."

God, I was a sucker for that pathetic voice. "What's your date of birth?"

"Why?"

"Because I'm going to need it to get your prisoner number to coordinate your release."

"You don't remember when my birthday is?"

"Yes, I do. I just want to be sure."

She confirmed the date.

"Do you know when you're getting arraigned?"

"I don't know anything. All I know is the people here are mean, I'm hungry, and it's freezing."

"You'll probably go before a judge tomorrow morning. That's when they'll set bail."

"You mean I'm going to be in here all night?"

"If you're lucky, you'll get out sometime tomorrow afternoon."

"Oh God," she sobbed again. "Is there anything else you can do?"

"Not really."

"Don't you know people?"

"My contacts aren't going to do you any good. Just sit tight and I'll get on this. Keep to yourself and stay out of trouble. And don't say anything to anyone. Do you understand?"

"Yes."

"Did you answer any questions when you were arrested?"

"I'm not stupid. I've watched enough cop shows not to talk to them."

"I'm sure JD knows a good attorney."

"You're not going to tell him, are you?"

"What was our deal? You stay out of trouble, and I keep your secret. You broke your end of the deal."

An automated voice said, "This call will end in 15 seconds."

"Thanks, Tyson," she whimpered before the call got disconnected.

I handed the land-line back to Madison who had been listening intently.

"You want to tell me what that was all about?" she demanded.

21

"What the hell were you thinking?" JD's angry voice crackled through my phone. I had come clean about Scarlett's overdose.

"I thought she'd get her shit together. Most people do after a scare like that. She made a promise."

JD grumbled to himself.

"That girl is a master manipulator," I said, making an excuse.

"You don't have to tell me. She puts on that pouty face and bats her eye-lashes, and she gets anything she wants."

"Exactly."

"Well, that little miscreant can spend a couple nights in jail as far as I'm concerned."

"You can't just leave her there."

"The hell I can't. A few days, maybe a couple weeks, might do her some good?"

There was a long pause.

"Goddammit," JD griped. "And I was having a good evening too."

"You know a good lawyer?" I asked.

"I know a few. Something tells me this is going to be expensive."

"Yep."

"Hopefully she kept her damn mouth shut."

"She said she did."

"I'm going to make some phone calls, see what I can find out. Maybe I can make this whole thing go away?" JD said, hopeful.

"I'll run up there with you in the morning, if you want?"

"Let me sleep on it. I seriously might let her sit there for a few days."

There was a pause.

"Are we good?" I asked.

"Yeah, yeah. But the next time she pulls a stunt like that, and you find out about it, you tell me ASAP!"

"Fair enough."

"Oh, I got a call from Ashley. She cracked another encrypted file. She said it looks like ledgers and accounting info—balance sheets, transaction reports, a list of inventory, etc."

"Anything interesting?" I asked.

"I don't know. I was going to get the file from her tomorrow. But it looks like my day might be full."

"I thought you weren't worried about the case anymore?"

"Something just isn't sitting right with me," JD said. "I've been thinking about it all evening."

"Me too."

I hung up, left *Diver Down,* and strolled back to the *Slick'n Salty.* I climbed up to the bridge deck and drank another beer and looked out over the marina. It was calm and quiet. A gentle breeze blew through my hair. I stewed on everything that had gone wrong lately, wondering how it was all going to get sorted out?

After I finished my beer, I climbed down and went to bed, hoping that in the morning things would be a little clearer.

I was probably asleep 45 minutes when I heard the aft hatch squeak. It took my brain a moment to process the sound. I knew it couldn't be Aria—and it was unlikely Agent Archer was making a booty call.

I reached for my pistol, and just as I did, the hatch to my stateroom flung open. A black pistol edged into the compartment. It had a suppressor attached to the end of the barrel, and the pistol was held by a man dressed in all black, wearing a ski mask.

Bullets zipped from the barrel as I rolled aside, crashing to the deck on the starboard side of the bed. Feathers fluttered in the air from my down pillow as a bullets tore through it.

I popped up and angled my pistol over the top of the bed and returned fire. Muzzle flash flickered.

Bang!

Bang!

Bang!

The deafening report rang my ears. I lost all hearing for a moment, leaving nothing but a high-pitched whine.

Bullets tore through fiberglass and wood paneling, and the haze of gun-smoke filled the air.

The assassin retreated. I heard his footsteps thud across the deck. The assassin scaled the transom and sprinted down the dock.

I raced through the salon and held up at the hatch, I whipped the barrel of my pistol around the corner and took aim at the assassin.

He craned his neck over his shoulder and fired two shots at me as he reached the end of the dock.

I ducked back into the salon as bullets impacted the bulkhead inches from where my head had been.

My heart thudded, and I took a deep breath.

I cautiously poked my head through the aft hatch again, but this time the assassin was gone.

Tires squealed, spitting gravel as the assassin peeled out of the parking lot and disappeared onto the highway.

The sound of my pulse rushed through my ears. The ringing had subsided, replaced by an annoying hiss, which was pretty much ever-present from my prolonged and consistent exposure to weapons fire.

I could hear just fine now, but I would probably be that old man who said *what* a lot and complained about his hearing aid—*if* I made it that long.

I had never locked the hatch when I was aboard the *Slick'n Salty*. Marinas were generally safe. There was a good sense of community. People looked out for each other. But I was beginning to think I should probably keep the boat locked up, even when I was aboard.

I stepped back into the galley and grabbed a bottle of water from the fridge. At least I knew one thing, the assassins that shot up the *Slick'n Salty* the other day weren't just after Agent Archer.

I looked at my watch. It was a little after two in the morning. I figured I better call Archer and warn her. After a few rings, her groggy voice answered, "What?"

"Somebody just tried to kill me."

"What?" she said again, this time her voice perkier.

I gave her the details.

"I just thought I'd call and let you know. You should watch your back."

"Thanks for the heads up," she replied. "So, were you alone on the boat?"

I could tell she was partially asking out of professional curiosity, and partially asking out of personal. "Yeah, it was just me."

"Did you get a look at the guy?"

"It was dark, and it happened fast. He wore a mask. Beyond that, I can't tell you much."

There was a long pause.

"I'll let you get back to sleep," I said.

She scoffed. "Like that's going to happen. I'm up for the rest of the night, now."

"Would you feel better if I came over?"

"Absolutely not!"

"I was only offering in a professional sense," I said. "I can call the Sheriff's Department, if you'd like a protection detail?"

"You don't have the resources, and I'm perfectly capable of taking care of myself."

"I have no doubt."

"Good night, Deputy Wild."

"Good night, Agent Archer."

I hung up the phone and called JD and told him to watch his back as well.

"Hell, I'd like to see them come around here," JD said. "They'll be in for a rude awakening."

"I'm getting the impression this case isn't as cold as we may have thought," I said.

"You took the words right out of my mouth."

"You know, maybe it's a good thing Scarlett's in jail. At least she's safer there."

"Ha. Right," JD grumbled. He thought for a moment. "I guess that's one way to look at it."

22

F BI agents from DC showed up bright and early in the morning. They asked a ton of questions, dug slugs out of the fiberglass hull, and took a statement from me.

I told them about the previous night's assassin, and they collected slugs from the stateroom as well. They were all business, and weren't exactly friendly.

Once they had left, I figured I would get some work done around the boat and wait to hear from JD. I gathered up a load of laundry that I'd been putting off, and stuffed it into a bag. I slung it over my shoulder and marched to *Diver Down* and asked Madison if I could use her washer and dryer.

Living full-time on a boat sounds great, but you give up a few conveniences. It's not much of a sacrifice, but you've got to haul groceries from the parking lot down the dock. There is usually a community cart to assist with such things, but it frequently goes missing. And you're constantly fighting mold and mildew, especially in the shower. All things considered, I was enjoying living on the boat, apart from the times when people shot at me. But with my history, that could happen anywhere.

My phone buzzed. I looked at the display. To my surprise, it was Aria.

"Hey," she said when I answered.

"Hey."

There was a long pause.

"I'm sorry I freaked out on you. I just didn't expect you to move on so quickly."

"I didn't move on. Things just... happened."

"I get it." She paused. "I feel like I made a complete mess of things. This is all my fault."

"You did what you felt you needed to do," I said, trying to be understanding.

"Listen, I don't have a lot of time to talk right now, but I miss you. I'd like to see you again. I have a pretty hectic schedule over the next month. I'm doing shoots almost every day. Maybe we can get together after that. Maybe we can go on vacation somewhere?"

"That sounds nice."

"I still don't expect you to do this long distance thing. So, whatever you need to do in between now and then, I just don't need to know about. I just want to be able to spend time with you, and I don't want it to be weird or filled with drama."

"Life's too short for unnecessary drama," I said.

She breathed a sigh of relief. "Whew. That's a load off my chest. I was feeling really... bad about the way we left things."

"Me too."

"Great!" She said, in a cheery voice. "I'll talk to you soon."

I wasn't about to pretend that I had the skill to actually decipher the meaning of our conversation. I've been around long enough to know that sometimes what is said is not what is meant. But it sounded to me like we didn't have any obligations to each other, and we would just see what happened when we got together next? But I had no idea when that would be, and I wasn't going to hold my breath.

I had finished a couple loads of laundry when JD called. "I have no willpower. I can't let her sit there for a few days. Do you want to ride up there with me?"

"Since I feel partly responsible, yes."

"Okay. I'll swing by in a few and pick you up."

JD showed up at the *Slick'n Salty* with a green ammo case. "Got any place to stow this?"

"What is it?" I asked, suspicious, knowing full well what it was.

"See for yourself."

I took the case and opened it. Inside were fragmentation grenades, still in their shipping canisters. "Where did you get these?"

"Fell off the back of a truck," JD said with a wink. "I'm trying to child-proof my home. I don't want anything walking off when that little dope-head gets back. I've locked up all my guns and valuables."

"You think she'd steal from you?"

"I didn't think she was using drugs. Caught me completely off guard. I'm not taking any chances. You could get a pretty penny for those on the market. Enough to feed a habit."

"You got an angle with a supply clerk somewhere?"

"I've got angles everywhere." JD grinned.

"What exactly do you plan on doing with these?"

"One can never have enough explosive devices. Besides, they might come in handy during the zombie apocalypse."

I rolled my eyes and put the case in a stowage compartment.

We raced up to Miami at a speed that would make a Formula One driver nervous. Wind raced through my hair, and the howl of the flat six roared. JD pumped the music, and it almost felt like a road trip. But this destination wouldn't be pleasant.

We were about halfway to Miami when red and blue lights flickered behind us.

JD pulled to the shoulder and made sure to display his badge when he handed the officer his driver's license and insurance.

"Is there an emergency or other reason for your excessive speed?" the highway patrolman said behind mirrored shades.

"My daughter is in the hospital in Miami. I'm trying to get there as quick as possible. We're not sure if she's going to make it."

The officer frowned. "I'm sorry to hear that. Be careful. I'll radio ahead that you're coming through so you won't experience any more delays."

"Thank you, sir," JD said.

"I'll keep your daughter in my thoughts and prayers."

JD could barely keep a straight face. He looked to me and grinned and winked as the officer started back to his patrol car.

Jack dropped it into gear, let out the clutch, and we were off to the races again.

"You've got nine lives, JD," I said.

Scarlett had been arraigned that morning and charged with possession of a controlled substance under Florida statute, 893.13 (6) (a). If convicted, she could face up to five years and a maximum fine of $5000.

JD had coordinated with a bondsman and an attorney. We just had to wait for Scarlett to get released.

The inmate release area was dingy and grimy and looked like it hadn't been cleaned since 1962. It took on all the wondrous odors of the people who came in and out—a mix of body odor, alcohol, smoke, and vomit.

When we arrived, the computers were down. So, we had to wait an additional two hours for her to get processed out.

When Scarlett was finally released, she looked like she'd been through the ringer. Her hair was frazzled, and her mascara had stained her cheeks from crying.

She was wearing a skimpy black dress from the night before, and who knows what happened to her shoes? The soles of her bare feet were black like coal, and she held an envelope in her hand that contained personal belongings—her watch, jewelry, credit cards, and money.

She ran into JD's arms and gave him a hug. "I'm so sorry, Dad."

She looked up at him with red puffy eyes. I'm sure her sad and pathetic and adorable face melted his heart, but he tried to be stern.

"You're not going to weasel your way out of this one with a sad face. You're in a lot of trouble, young lady!"

"It's not my fault."

"Save the bullshit for someone else."

We left the station, and Scarlett climbed into the backseat of JD's 911. If you've ever been in a 911, you know there isn't much of a backseat.

"Can we get something to eat?" Scarlett asked. "The food in there sucks."

"I should let you starve," JD grumbled.

He cranked up the engine, and we peeled out of the parking lot.

"Where do you want to eat?" JD asked.

"Anywhere," Scarlett said.

We stopped at *Chucky Burger* and had cheeseburgers. We were all pretty famished. We sat in a booth and devoured our meal, and no one said much of anything until near the end.

"Tomorrow you're going to rehab," JD said.

Scarlett's face went pale, and her eyes nearly popped out of their sockets. "What?"

"It's all set up. It's a 28 day program."

"No. I don't need to go to rehab. I'm not a drug addict."

"Let's see... You overdosed, and you got arrested, all in the span of one week. I'd say you've got a problem."

She glared at him, her face turning red. "I do not have a problem!"

"I beg to differ. You've got quite a few. It's real simple. You go to rehab, follow the program, or I stop paying for your attorney, and you can take your chances with the public defender."

She huffed.

"Take your pick. 28 days, or five years?"

"This is SO not fair."

"You're right," JD said. "It's totally not fair. I shouldn't have to drive up here and pull you out of jail. You're smart enough to know better."

Scarlett shifted her gaze to me. Her eyes were like lasers. "I can't believe you told him."

"It was part of the deal," I said.

"You are so not my favorite person anymore."

JD looked at me. "This is gratitude. Now I'm convinced we should have left her in there."

"I've been through a traumatic experience. You don't need to be an asshole, Jack."

It was the wrong thing to say to JD. "I'm the asshole? You'd better be careful. You are way, *way*, out of line."

She gritted her teeth and glared at him as she slid out of the booth and stormed out of the restaurant.

"Ungrateful little..." He stopped short of calling her a bitch.

"Maybe go a little easier on her. She *did* spend the night in jail."

"Oh, hell no! Her little manipulative act might work on you, but I'm all stocked up here."

JD took his time finishing his meal. He paid the tab, and when we strolled to the parking lot, Scarlett was leaning against the car with her arms folded.

Her eyes threw daggers at JD, and the two didn't speak the entire way home. It was about 10:30 PM by the time we got back to *Diver Down*.

I climbed out of the car.

Before Jack sped off, he said, "Remind me to have Ashley send you that encrypted file. Maybe you can look it over tonight?"

"Sure thing."

"Thanks for coming to get me, Tyson," Scarlett said as she slipped out of the back and into the front passenger seat.

"What about me?" JD said. "Don't I get a little bit of thanks?"

She turned away, still not talking to him.

23

"Wow!" Dean Melville said.

He stood on the dock, staring at the *Slick'n Salty,* his jaw slack, and his eyes wide. "You said a *few* bullet holes."

I shrugged. "Yeah, a few."

"That's considerably more than a few."

"Can you fix it?"

Dean had dark curly hair, brown eyes, a round belly, and a day's worth of stubble on his face. He was mid 30s, and THE guy to go to for boat repair on the island. "I'm surprised this thing is still floating."

"I don't think there's much damage under the water line."

Dean rubbed his chin. "I can fix it. But it ain't going to be cheap."

"Take a look and give me an estimate."

Dean climbed the transom and surveyed the cockpit, taking note of the number of bullet holes and the damage. He scribbled on to his small spiral pad.

It was 10 AM, and the morning sun cascaded over the Marina. Gulls squawked overhead.

Dean groaned as he entered the salon. The wood paneling was pocked and splintered. "Remind me to never let you borrow one of my boats. Who the hell did you piss off?"

"An ex-girlfriend. She didn't like how things ended."

He let out a nervous chuckle, not sure if I was joking.

Dean finished surveying the boat and said he'd get back to JD with an estimate. In the meantime, he recommended diving around the hull and inspecting for damage.

Shortly after he left, Ashley called. She sent me a download link for the data files she had decrypted. I was able to open them on my phone and peruse the spreadsheets. There was a lot of data about Scott Kingston's business.

One of the files contained a list of HINs (hull identification numbers). Much like the VIN number on a car, these identification numbers were used to track the history of the boat.

This particular document contained the original HIN number alongside a new number. Kingston had clearly been taking stolen boats and retitling them. The list contained thousands of boats, along with a record of whom the stolen boats were sold to. There was also a column of initials next to each HIN. I assumed this might be the initials of the criminal the boat was acquired from?

I was quite sure the purchasers had no idea they were buying stolen property.

It sent my mind swirling with ideas. I jogged down the dock to *Diver Down* and looked for Madison. I found her behind the bar. "Hey, do you still have Dad's files?"

"What do you need?"

"The title on the boat. Anything that might have the HIN number like insurance documents, registration, etc."

Her face twisted, not sure where I was going with this. "I'm pretty sure I kept all that stuff. Why?"

"I just want to check on something."

"Watch the bar. I'll go look in my files."

I slipped around the counter and played bartender for 15 minutes.

Madison returned with the title. "Have you found something?"

I don't know." I looked at the HIN number, then searched the list. For a match.

I found one.

The boat had been sold to Rory Tilman a month after my parents' disappearance.

It was purchased from someone with the initials XC.

My body tensed, and anger boiled within me. I was now on a mission to find XC. If this person didn't kill my parents, they might be able to tell me who did.

Madison cried when I told her the connection. Her tears

were a mix of sadness, anger, and hope. She wrapped her arms around me and gave me a hug.

It was unexpected.

She sobbed on my shoulder for a moment, and I put a comforting arm around her.

"I'll find out who did this." I assured her.

I went back to the boat and continued studying the files. I noticed some anomalies in the accounting reports. I studied the transaction receipts, invoices, assets, liabilities, cost of goods sold, and inventory reports.

Scott Kingston was up to something that just may have gotten him killed.

24

It was a complicated scheme of false sales receipts, over-inflated loan payments, transaction reports for merchandise that never existed, and payables to an offshore supplier. Kingston had failed to file cash transaction reports for amounts over $10,000, and if he would have been caught, he would probably have spent the rest of his life behind bars.

Becoming a Confidential Informant for the FBI had taken the heat off him. But my guess is that made some of his business partners extremely nervous. To top it off, it looked like he was skimming some of the profits.

I called JD. "I think I found something. There's a shell company in the Cayman Islands that Kingston was making large payments to. *Votraxx Industries*. If we can find out who is behind that company, we might be one step closer."

"I'll see what I can find out. I'm a little busy at the moment." His voice was thick with concern.

"What's going on?"

"I was going to take Scarlett into rehab today. But she's not here. She took off in the middle of the night. I've been trying to track her down."

"Have you checked with her friends? That former boyfriend of hers?"

"Yeah. They don't know where she is. Or they aren't saying. I haven't been able to get hold of Chloe. I spoke with her parents, and they don't know anything. They blame Scarlett. Say she's a bad influence."

"We'll find her," I assured.

"I'm worried about her. God knows where she is, or what she's doing."

"We should let Sheriff Daniels know. Put out an APB."

"Running away and not going to rehab is not illegal, Tyson. I can't legally make her do anything. She's an adult. She's fully capable of making her own decisions. Even if they are bad ones."

"If I can find her, maybe I can talk some sense into her."

"Good luck." He paused. "She does seem to respect you more than she respects me. Who knows. Maybe she might listen?"

"She's going to be okay. She's just going through a phase."

"Her whole life has been a phase." He changed the subject. "Oh, hey. Dean called with an estimate. I think I'm going to sell the boat as is."

That hung in the air like smoke.

"Really?"

"He does good work, but he's slow as hell. The *Slick'n Salty* could be out of commission for a month or more. And he needs to custom order those panel replacements. That's 6 to 8 weeks at least. That's a lot of downtime. No charters. Which means no revenue. Scarlett's legal fees aren't going to be cheap either. With the attorney I've hired to defend this case, I'm looking at $50K."

"I guess I should start looking for another residence."

"You can always crash on the couch here. And if that little miscreant goes to jail, I'll have an available room." It was a desperate attempt to lighten the situation.

I had grown to like living on the boat, and I wasn't thrilled about the prospect of losing my residence. But I didn't really have any say in the matter.

"Chloe works at *Breakwater*," I said. "I'll stop by and see if I can learn anything."

"I'd appreciate that."

"I'll keep in touch." I hung up the phone.

I went to *Breakwater* and talked to the manager. He said that Chloe's shift was supposed to start at 4 PM, but she missed the last two days because she was *sick*.

I gave it 50-50 odds of her showing up. I went back to the boat and planned to come back to *Breakwater* later.

Agent Archer was walking down the dock away from the *Slick'n Salty* when I arrived. I was surprised to see her. "What are you doing here?"

"I just wanted to stop by and say thank you for giving me a

heads up the other night. I felt like I came across a little bit... rude."

"Maybe a little."

She glared at me playfully.

"I take it no trouble?"

She shrugged. "I thought I picked up a tail the other day. But, I can't be sure. I'm definitely looking over my shoulder."

"I know the feeling."

"Have you found out anything new?" she asked.

"Votraxx Industries," I said.

Her face twisted.

"See if you can find out who owns that company."

I filled her in on the details.

"I think Kingston was laundering money for some heavy hitters. I also think he was taking a little more of the profits than he should have been."

"And you think that's why he was killed?"

"Could be. Or it could be they thought he was going to snitch."

"Look, we got Kingston on a possession charge. We leaned on him pretty hard, and he offered to cooperate by giving us a heads up on anyone he thought was moving a large amount of product in the area. In exchange we made the Federal charges go away."

"And that created an opportunity for him to go into business with someone else and put his competition out of business.."

"It happens," Archer conceded.

"As long as you make your quota, right?"

Her eyes narrowed at me. "I don't care about quotas. You know why I am doing this."

"Sorry," I said.

There was an awkward pause.

"You got time for lunch?"

She thought about it for a moment. She didn't want to seem too eager. "If you're buying?"

We got a table on the patio at *Diver Down*. There was a cool breeze, and the midday sun glimmered across the water. The boats in the marina gently rocked, and seagulls drifted on the wind.

Kim took our order. I ordered the calamari and the crawfish étouffée, and Archer started with a Mediterranean salad and grilled shrimp.

"You know I'm still doing paperwork and answering follow-up questions from the incident," she said.

"I'm not surprised."

"I'm sorry about your boat."

"JD's boat. And it looks like he decided to sell it."

She made a sad face. "Oh, no. What are you going to do?"

I shrugged. "I guess I'll have to get a real apartment." I

thought about it for a moment. "Who knows,? Maybe I'll buy a boat of my own?"

"And how are you going to afford that? It's not like volunteer deputies are flush with cash." She thought about it for moment. "Speaking of which, how does JD afford that boat?"

"He did okay as a private contractor. He invested well and got lucky with a few tech and biomedical stocks. He keeps his cards close to his chest. He always acts like he's broke, but I think he's got more than he lets on. I don't know too many broke guys who drive Porsches."

"What about you?"

"Getting nosy, aren't you?" I said, playfully.

"Well, I've looked into your background as much as I can. And I still don't have a lot of answers. You must have been somebody special within the *Company*."

"Are you calling me a has-been?"

She smiled.

"I prefer the term, retired."

Kim returned with our appetizers. She set them on the table, and the smell of the fried calamari hit my nostrils. I suddenly realized I was hungrier than I had anticipated.

"Can I get you anything else?" Kim asked.

"No, thanks," I said.

"You're entrées will be out shortly." She spun around and sauntered away.

I attacked the calamari, and Archer dug into her salad.

"So, tell me about your girlfriend?" she said casually, letting it drip from her lips as if it were no big deal.

I sighed. "I told you, I don't have a girlfriend."

"I don't know. Do non-girlfriends always fly in from out of town and surprise you in the middle of the night?"

"I thought it was none of your business?"

"It's not. I was just wondering," she said, trying to act disinterested. "You know, I would hate for that situation to happen again."

I lifted a curious eyebrow. "Again?"

She shrugged. Well, I mean. Let's be honest. The sex wasn't... horrible."

"Not horrible?"

"I mean, it may have been a little better than I let on."

"A little?"

"Okay. Maybe a *little* is not a good word in this context?"

"Thank you." I still wasn't sure where she was going with this.

Her cheeks flushed, and she fidgeted nervously. She looked like she was starting to sweat. She fanned herself with her hand. "It's a little hot out here, isn't it?"

"What are you getting at?"

"I'm just saying. I work a lot. Long hours. Stressful situations. It's not really conducive to a relationship." Then she stammered, "So, I was thinking maybe we could have a... friends with benefits type arrangement?"

"Benefits?" I said. "You mean, like a 401(k)?"

She was uncomfortable, and I wanted to see her squirm.

Her eyes narrowed at me.

"If you're not interested, I'm sure I can find someone else who's more than willing to satisfy my needs."

"I didn't say I wasn't interested."

"Good. It's settled." She smiled and went back to her salad like we had been talking about the weather.

"So, what are the rules?"

"Rules?"

"Yeah, because, you know, these things have a tendency to get... sticky."

"If done correctly," she said with a devious grin.

"You know what I mean."

She paused and took a deep breath. "Okay. I'm not stupid. You're a good looking guy, and I know you have a lot of options. I don't want to get hurt. So I'm not even going to put that on the table. You want rules? I'll give you rules. No feelings. No *L* words. No surprise visits. No jealousy. No questions. We do this as long as it's fun. And we call it off when one of us loses interest. No big deal."

I looked at her, astonished. "And I don't have to pay you?"

She scowled at me playfully and smacked my bicep with her palm. "Like I said, if you don't think you can handle an arrangement like that, I'm happy to find some other guy with a big dick that can."

"I don't have any objections. I'm all aboard, Captain." I paused for a moment, then added. "You said big."

Her eyes narrowed at me. "Do not get cocky."

I flashed a confident grin. I felt like I had died and gone to *no commitment* heaven. It sounded too good to be true. These situations rarely worked in the long term, but it would be an interesting ride for a while.

Kim returned with our entrées. "Enjoy your meal."

25

Reggae music filtered through the air as I stepped into *Breakwater*. I had waited until the evening to stop by and see if Chloe had made it to work. The afternoon crowd was thinning out, and the late night crowd hadn't arrived yet. I took a seat at a cocktail table near the bar. Within a few minutes, a waitress sauntered up and asked for my order.

"Is Chloe here?"

"Yeah, I think so. You want me to send her over?"

"Please."

"Sure thing." She spun around and sauntered away.

A few moments later, Chloe approached the table. We had met a few times before, but I wasn't sure she'd recognize me out of context. She had platinum blonde hair, blue eyes, and full lips. "Drinking alone tonight?"

"Actually, I'm looking for Scarlett."

Her smile faded. "I don't know where she is."

"I think you do."

"Maybe I do. Maybe I don't. But I don't have to tell you."

She started to turn away but I stopped her. I put a $100 bill on the table. "You haven't taken my drink order yet."

She huffed, and her eyes narrowed at me. "What do you want?"

"Service with a smile?" I asked tentatively.

She forced a smile, but her eyes threw daggers. "If Scarlett's your friend, you'll let me help her."

"You guys are making way too much of a deal out of this."

"You both got arrested and charged with felony possession. That's a pretty big deal."

She looked around, a little embarrassed. "Why don't you say that louder? I don't think anybody else heard you."

"Tell me where Scarlett is and you can keep the change."

"I don't need your money."

"With the charges you're facing, I think you could use every penny you can get your hands on. Legal fees aren't cheap."

"I didn't do anything wrong. It wasn't mine. And my parents are paying my legal fees." Her snotty face crinkled with irritation.

"Okay. I'll play along. So it wasn't yours. Where'd you get it?"

"I'm not saying anything without my attorney. I mean, you're a cop, aren't you?"

"Deputy Sheriff. It's temporary."

"Then I am definitely not talking to you."

She spun around and stormed away, leaving my crisp clean hundred dollar bill on the table top.

I watched as she moved to the bar and spoke with her manager. She pointed in my direction, and I knew what was coming next. The big guy strolled toward me with an angry face. He was a barrel chested man that looked like he'd thrown his fair share of patrons out of the bar. He towered over me. "My waitress says you're harassing her."

"Just asking a few questions."

"She says you grabbed her ass. I think it's time for you to get out of here before I call the cops."

I felt like now was the appropriate time to flash my badge.

"Do you drug test your employees here?"

"No. This is a bar. I don't care what they do on their free time. But I'll make sure she files a complaint with your department."

"I'm sure they'll take the word of an accused felon over mine."

His face scrunched up. "Accused felon?"

"Didn't she tell you. The reason she hasn't been at work for the last few days is because she was arrested for possession of cocaine."

He grimaced and looked over his shoulder at her.

"If I were you, I'd be careful who you hire. Cash has a habit of going missing around addicts." I smiled. "Have a nice evening."

I pushed away from the table and strolled toward the exit.

I stepped out of the bar and onto the sidewalk and waited for a moment, watching the tourists walk up and down the crowded avenue, hopping from bar to bar. It was a week-night, so there wasn't as much traffic as on the weekends. But Coconut Key was a tourist destination—there were always crowds. There were always people looking to blow off steam.

Five minutes later, Chloe emerged from the bar, wiping the tears from her eyes. Her face was red and puffy. Rage boiled in her veins the moment she saw me. She marched to me and smacked me in the arm. "You got me fired, you fucking asshole!"

I admit, it was kind of a dick move, but I needed answers from her. "You just assaulted an officer."

Her face twisted with anger. "What?"

"You just hit me. That is assault and battery."

"What's the matter? You can't take a punch from a girl?"

"Tell me where I can find Scarlett, and you don't spend another night in jail."

She clenched her jaw and growled through gritted teeth. "I hate you!"

"Where is she?"

"She's with Justin. On his boat, *Miss Conduct*."

I rolled my eyes. "Where?"

"Pirates Cove. Happy?"

I smiled. "See. Wasn't that easy?"

"I hope you get hit by a bus." She scowled at me and stormed away.

I chuckled. "It was nice talking to you."

She craned her neck over her shoulder, gave me a dirty look, and raised her middle finger.

26

I strolled down the dock at Pirates Cove, looking for *Miss Conduct*. Boats creaked, and riggings clanked.

I caught sight of Justin's boat. It was a 40 foot performance sailboat—a Vanguard X-144. It was sleek and refined, and had luxurious live-aboard accommodations. Its hull was infusion molded. It was a cruiser/racer and couldn't have been more than a few years old. It was easily a $500,000 boat, and if I had to wager a guess, Justin's father had bought it for him.

Amber light filtered through portals in the main cabin. The muffled sound of music echoed across the marina, along with voices.

I heard Scarlett.

I stood on the dock beside the port side of the sailboat and called to her. "Scarlett. It's Tyson. Can you come out here?"

The voices stopped.

There was a long pause.

"Scarlett, I know you're in there."

A few moments later, the hatch opened, and Scarlett poked her head out. "What are you doing here?"

"What do you think I'm doing here?"

"I'm not going to rehab. He can't make me go."

"No, but if you voluntarily check yourself into a rehab facility, stay on the straight and narrow, maybe your attorney could get a good plea deal?"

"I told you. It wasn't mine."

"Okay. For the sake of argument. Let's say it wasn't yours. That's irrelevant. You've been charged. And you'll have to fight it. I don't think you're quite aware of what's ahead of you. And how this could impact the rest of your life."

She rolled her eyes.

"It's a felony, Scarlett. You won't be able to vote."

"So, they all suck anyway."

"You won't be able to own a gun. You'll have a hard time getting jobs. It will follow you forever."

Justin slid past her and stepped into the cockpit. "Hey, buddy. I think she made it pretty clear that she doesn't want you here. She can make her own decisions. Why don't you get lost?"

My body tensed, and I bit my tongue. This punk kid was maybe 19 or 20. I probably shouldn't smack him. "Justin, is it?"

"What part of get the fuck out of here did you not understand?" he barked.

"I don't remember involving you in this discussion. So why don't you go back into the cabin and let me and Scarlett talk this out?"

"I'm getting sick of listening to you yammer." He stepped to the port gunwale, puffing his chest, staring me down, attempting to be some kind of bad ass.

He was a muscular guy. Fit. Athletic.

But he had no clue what he was getting himself into. He flashed his perfect teeth and had a cocky grin on his lips. "I'm gonna tell you one more time to leave. If you don't. Things are gonna get ugly."

"You're goddamn right they are."

"Justin, let me talk to him," Scarlett said.

"I'm done talking," Justin said.

He reached under his shirt and pulled a pistol from his waistband and aimed it at my head. His hand trembled slightly as the rush of adrenaline washed through his body. "Still want to talk to Scarlett?"

"Why don't you put the gun away before you get hurt."

The muscles in his jaw flexed. Even with the gun, he was an insecure loser.

"Okay. Fine. I'm gone," I said, raising my hands, innocently.

He relaxed slightly, and I took the opportunity to strike. Like lightning I grabbed the barrel with one hand and his forearm with the other. I twisted the weapon 180°, snapping his finger in the trigger guard. In a flash, I had the weapon in my possession. He whined like a little bitch and doubled over.

I pressed the mag release button, dropped the magazine into my palm, and tossed it into the water. Then I ejected the round from the chamber. It clattered against the deck, and rolled into the abyss. "Why don't you take a walk and let me finish my conversation?"

Scarlett stared with wide eyes, her hands over her mouth.

Justin decided to get brave. He stood up and swung a left hook. He had some power behind his punch. It would have hurt, if it had connected. But his fist whooshed an inch in front of my nose.

I grabbed his forearm pulling him aside, while simultaneously hammering a fist into his rib cage.

He groaned as the air escaped his lungs, and his torso twisted around my fist. Then I planted an elbow into his nose. Bones crackled, and blood splattered.

He wailed in pain as he dropped to the deck, crimson blood speckling the white fiberglass hull.

"Permission to come aboard?" I asked, mockingly. I lifted my finger to my ear and bent it. "Permission granted? Thank you."

I climbed over the gunwale as Justin writhed on the deck. I took Scarlett by the arm. "We're leaving."

She glared at me for a moment. "Okay. Wait. I need to get my purse."

She ducked back into the cabin. I stood by the hatch,

watching her as she grabbed a small clutch and stepped back to the cockpit. I helped her off the boat and marched her down the dock.

I called JD and told him to pick us up. We waited in the parking lot.

Scarlett fidgeted nervously. She sniffled and rubbed her nose several times.

I looked into her eyes. "Are you high?"

"No."

My eyes narrowed at her. I gave her a look that said you better start telling me the truth.

"Maybe a little."

I deflated, disappointed. "What happened, Scarlett? Why are you doing this to yourself?"

"I don't know." Her eyes brimmed. She threw her arms around me and sobbed. "I'm sorry, Tyson."

"Don't apologize to me. Apologize to your dad."

A few minutes later, JD's red Porsche pulled into the parking lot, and the engine purred alongside us. I had never seen JD look so relieved in his entire life.

I held the door open for Scarlett and she slipped into the passenger seat.

"I was worried sick about you," JD said.

"I'm sorry," her eyes still wet and growing wetter.

The two hugged each other.

"I'm taking you right now to the facility. I called ahead. They're waiting for us. Everything's gonna be fine."

Scarlett nodded.

JD's concerned eyes flicked to me. "I owe you one, brother."

"No, you don't."

27

I caught a cab back to *Diver Down*. There were a few regulars, and a handful of tourists. I took a seat at the bar and ordered a whiskey.

"Any luck with Scarlett?" Madison asked.

"Yeah. I found her. JD's taking her to rehab now."

Madison breathed a sigh of relief. "That's great. I hope she can get her shit together."

"Me too."

"Look, I'm sorry I gave you a bunch of shit earlier."

"It's okay. I'm used to you having a low opinion of me."

She gasped. "That's not true."

"Yes it is."

She squinted at me. "Okay, maybe I said a few things that I shouldn't have. Jumped to conclusions prematurely."

I reveled in her pseudo-apology with a cocksure grin on my

face.

"Have you found out anything more about Mom and Dad?"

"No. I've had my hands full. But if I can find out who XC is, maybe that will bring me closer."

"What about the person who bought the boat?"

"That could have been a falsified sales receipt. Besides, it would be unlikely that he had any knowledge of where the boat came from."

"It might be worth a shot. Leave no stone unturned."

"Yes, boss."

I sat at the bar, sipping whiskey, watching the people, going over Kingston's case in my mind. Everywhere I went, I was looking over my shoulder.

I always made sure I took a seat where I could see the entrance. I plotted my exit routes. Looked for cover. Watched for anyone suspicious. It was standard operating procedure for me. But knowing that someone was out there trying to kill me, made me a little more vigilant. Over time, it made even mundane activities seem exhausting.

"You still keep a shotgun handy under the bar?" I asked.

Madison nodded.

"I want you to start carrying 24/7. You've still got Dad's Sig, right?"

"Yeah. What's going on?"

"I don't want to alarm you, or anything, but..."

"Okay, that's alarming. The very fact that you have to preface your next sentence with that is causing me concern."

"There have been two attempts on my life."

Her eyes widened. "Recently? Why didn't you say something earlier?"

"I don't know. I didn't want to freak you out."

She huffed. "I'm a little freaked out."

"Relax. I've got everything under control."

"No you don't. We just went through this. I'm not ready for this again."

"Just keep your weapon with you at all times, and have good situational awareness."

"Am I in danger?"

"Danger is a relative term. I mean riding in a car, flying in a plane, walking on the street... all dangerous."

She scowled at me.

"You are way more likely to die on a bicycle then you are from a homicide."

"I don't have a bike," she growled.

"See. Nothing to worry about."

She clenched her jaw, and I could tell she wanted to spit fire at me. "Is this what it's going to be like with you living around here? Constant chaos? All the time?"

"I promise, I don't go looking for it."

"Yes you do. You thrive on chaos."

Madison had enough of the conversation. She spun around and tended to patrons on the other end of the bar.

Maybe she was right? Maybe I purposely made decisions that put me into chaotic situations? Maybe I was afraid of boredom? Or maybe I just shouldn't try to psychoanalyze myself?

I got a text from Agent Archer. It read: *[Want to punch my benefit card?]*

I replied, *Sure. Want to grab a drink?*

[No. It's a school night. Come over and clock in.]

So, I'm on the job?

[Yes. There will be a performance evaluation afterward].

I chuckled. *I'll be there in 20.*

Agent Archer answered the door wearing a sheer négligée and smoldering eyes. The translucent fabric left nothing to the imagination. Her perfect curves and perky assets made my heart beat a little faster.

Agent Archer grabbed my shirt, balled her fingers into a fist, and pulled me into the foyer. Our lips collided, and we embraced passionately.

She wasn't wasting any time.

I kicked the door shut behind me as we melted into each other. Sensual music filtered through the air. Scented candles flickered, bathing the house in a soothing amber glow.

My hands traced the curves of her body.

When we broke for air, Archer took my hand and led me to the bedroom. "It's been a long day. I need a back rub, and possibly a foot massage."

"Okay."

"And afterward, you have to cuddle for at least an hour."

"An hour?" I asked.

"You didn't think this was going to be free, did you? I mean, you're going to have to work for it a little."

I smiled. "I don't mind work. Especially this kind."

"Good.

In the bedroom, she let the straps of the négligée fall from her shoulders. The frilly garment fluttered down, drifting over her supple curves, pooling at her ankles on the floor. She stepped out of it and climbed onto the bed like a cat.

She had my full attention.

"There's massage oil on the nightstand."

I proceeded to get undressed, then I grabbed the massage oil and squirted her back with a squiggly line of slippery oil. My hands caressed her smooth skin, working out her tense muscles. Her body relaxed, and a delicate moan escaped her full lips.

It wasn't long before the massage transformed into something even more pleasurable.

We performed our contractual obligations with vigor and passion. Our bodies collided. It was hot and sweaty and sweet and dirty, and when it was all said and done, I collapsed beside her, spooning her.

I held her close and caressed her silky form. I kissed the back of her neck and nuzzled her ear. "I think I could get used to this arrangement."

"Keep performing like that, and I might be inclined to extend our contract." She had a blissful smile on her face. She reached a delicate hand out and stroked my face. "You don't have to stay here tonight, but you're more than welcome."

"Does an overnight stay come with a complimentary breakfast?" I asked, playfully.

"It might," she said. "But if I'm going to cook for you in the morning, you might have to work for it."

"I think that can be arranged."

I dozed off with her warm body beside me.

The doorbell woke me up in the morning. I peeled my eyes open as the amber rays of sun filtered in through the blinds. I reached my hand out, feeling for Jen, but the bed was empty.

I heard the shower running.

My eyes flicked to the clock. It was 8:30 AM.

The bell rang again.

I climbed out of bed and pulled on my shorts, then stumbled through the living room toward the door. I pulled it open to see Tommy—the kid that lived across the street. I squinted from the bright light, still not fully adjusted.

He looked a little stunned to see me. "Is Jen here?"

"She's in the shower. What do you need?"

"She asked me to take a look at her car."

"Hang on. Let me go get her. I stepped away from the door, and headed back into the bedroom. I banged on the bathroom door and let Jen know Tommy was here.

She shut off the faucet, and the shower dripped. A few minutes later, she emerged from the bathroom amid a puff of steam with a towel wrapped around her torso. She fumbled through her purse on the dresser and found her keys and gave them to me. "Tell him it's making a clunking sound when I make a hard right turn."

"Sounds like a strut," I said.

"I don't know what that is."

I chuckled and went back to the front door and relayed the information to Tommy.

He agreed it sounds like a strut. "I'll spin around the block and see if I can reproduce the sound. If she wants, I can drive her to work, then take the car into my dad's shop. If it's something simple, I can probably have it ready by the time she gets off work."

"I'm sure she'll be fine with that."

I handed him the keys and he strolled toward the car. I closed the door and I heard the chirp of the alarm a second later.

Archer rounded the corner into the entrance foyer, and I told her what Tommy had said.

That's when it happened.

28

K ABOOM!

The ground rumbled, and the walls quaked. The windows shattered, spraying shards of glass in all directions. The blast knocked the front door from its hinges, and the overpressure sent me crashing to the ground on top of Archer.

I felt like I had been hit by a Mack truck.

I shook it off, sprang to my feet, and moved to what used to be the front door. Black smoke wafted into the air, and a blazing fire engulfed Archer's car. It crackled and popped. Metal pinged as it heated.

There was no way Tommy survived the blast.

The heat coming off the car was like a blowtorch. Debris littered the driveway and front lawn—twisted bits of sheet-metal, engine components, and hoses.

Archer's face contorted, and she shrieked with horror at the sight. Her eyes welled, and tears streamed down her cheeks.

She wanted to dart toward the car, but I held her back. There was nothing she could do. There was nothing anybody could do.

The smell of gasoline filled the air, along with the scent of burning rubber. The thick black smoke was noxious.

Before long, the area was teeming with FBI agents, firefighters, arson investigators, and forensics teams.

Archer sat on the couch in a stupor, wearing a robe. I recounted the details to Sheriff Daniels, and the FBI agents.

FBI Agent Miller stepped into the house, holding a small charred device. "This is the culprit. Car bomb. Wired into the ignition. We won't know until we get the chemical analysis back, but it was most likely C-4."

"Can you run the design through the database and see if you've encountered any other similar devices?" I asked.

"We can try," Miller said. He didn't seem thrilled to talk to me. "Like I said, once we get the chemical analysis back, we'll know more. We'll be able to tell if the explosive is homemade, or if it was military grade. It looks like a fairly standard design, but every bomb maker leaves their signature. Like a fingerprint."

"But the creator could be trying to mimic someone else's style," I said.

"Its possible," Agent Miller said, skeptical. "But lets not get ahead of ourselves."

Miller had dark hair, brown eyes, and was around 5'11. The air between us was tense, and he kept glaring at me.

"We can talk about this later, if you prefer, Agent Archer?" Daniels said.

"No. I'm fine. I just... Tommy didn't deserve this."

"Nobody deserves something like this," Daniels said.

The FBI agents milled about, conferring with one another.

Daniels pulled me aside. "Do you think this has something to do with the Kingston case?"

"Absolutely. Somebody doesn't want us on this case."

"Have you got any concrete leads?" "

"Nothing concrete," I said. "Not yet."

"I'd say you're probably getting pretty close." Daniels said. "You tell me what you want to do. I understand completely if you want to back away from this."

I looked at him like he was crazy. "I never back down. This kind of shit just pisses me off."

"When I asked you to come in on this, I never thought it would get this complicated. I thought it would be simple and by the numbers."

"Nothing is ever simple."

Archer got dressed and left with the investigating agents and went to the field office.

I stuck around her place and cleaned up the mess after everyone had gone. I caught an Uber to a home improve-ment store and got some heavy mill drop-cloth and duct tape and used it to seal off the broken windows and the front door. It wouldn't do much to deter a criminal, but it would keep the bugs out.

I called several different door companies and got estimates on replacing the front door. Let me tell you, a good door isn't cheap, and there's a 6 to 7 week lead time.

I went back to the home improvement store and found a 36 inch door with the same in-swing. It was in stock. It wasn't much to look at—just a white metal door—but it would do the job until a more permanent replacement could be installed. It was $400, and for an extra $150, they'd deliver that afternoon.

When I got back to Archer's place, I used a prybar to pull off the trim around the door frame, and I started demoing the area. By the time the door arrived, I had the area prepped. It took me another several hours to get it installed and sealed. By the time Archer got back late that evening, the new door opened and closed and locked. The flat white color didn't look as nice as a stained wood finish, but it got the job done.

Archer looked astonished. "Did you do that yourself?"

"No. I had little elves come in and fix it up."

Her eyes narrowed at me.

"This is just a temporary solution," I said.

"Thank you. Wasn't expecting this. This goes above and beyond our agreement." She smiled.

I shrugged, modestly. "Well, you know, I like happy clients."

"I'm anything but happy. But that's not your fault. She stepped into the living room and plopped onto the couch, tossing her purse aside. She let out a deep breath.

"Need a drink?"

"Two. Maybe three," she said.

I moved into the kitchen, uncorked a bottle of Pinot Noir, and poured a glass. I brought it to her in the living room.

"Now this is what I call service." She took a sip, then set the glass on the coffee table. "Durant has taken me off the case."

"Really? That's your boss, I assume?"

She nodded. "Says I'm too close."

"So what now?"

"He wants me to take a vacation, preferably out of the area. He's concerned for my safety."

"That's probably not a bad idea."

"Are you trying to get rid of me?" she asked.

"Not at all."

"Good."

"What's up with Agent Miller? Does he always have a stick up his ass? Or did he have a particular disdain for me?"

Archer hesitated a moment. "We went out a few times. Nothing serious."

"That explains why he was giving me the evil eye."

"He wasn't very happy about the way things ended."

"How did they end?"

"I really don't want to get into it right now. But, I just felt like he was always hiding something. I've got no time for games.

And he was a little too... controlling." She thought about it. "Needy. He'd freak if I didn't respond to his texts right away."

She shivered, shaking the memory of him away. "Ugh, what was I thinking. He's not even cute."

Archer sat there for a moment and had another sip of her wine. Then her eyes filled with tears again. The dam broke. She'd been holding her emotions back all day. She sniffled as she wiped the tears away. "I feel so bad about Tommy. It breaks my heart. He was such a good kid. I'm sure his parents hate me."

I sat next to her and put my arm around her. She leaned into me and slumped on my shoulder as I tried to comfort her.

29

"You don't have to stay here tonight if you don't want to," Archer said. "I'll be fine. Durant is sending two agents to watch the house."

"I don't mind staying," I said. "I never did get my breakfast."

"I'll be sure to make you a nice one tomorrow. That was really sweet what you did around here. It would totally have sucked to come home to a house with no front door and no windows."

"I've been wearing the same clothes since last night. Why don't you come back to the boat with me so I can get changed?"

We caught a cab over to the marina.

The FBI agents on protection detail hadn't arrived yet, so we were on our own.

I scanned the parking lot as the cab dropped us off at *Diver Down*. There were a few cars in the lot. The mercury vapor lights buzzed overhead, and I suddenly felt a little too exposed. These people weren't going to stop until we were dead, or had lost interest in the case.

We strolled down the dock toward the *Slick'n Salty*. The air was quiet and still. Water lapped against the hulls of the boats. I suddenly had that feeling in my gut that something was wrong. The hairs on the back of my neck stood tall, like they had always done before walking into an ambush or a bad situation.

About that time, Archer put a hand on my arm, stopping my forward progression. I flashed her a curious look.

"If they booby-trapped my car, what's to say they haven't done the same thing to your boat?"

She had a good point.

I scaled the transom and moved forward along the gunwale. The plastic covering I had placed over the broken window rippled in the breeze. I peeled it aside and peered into the salon, checking to see if the hatch had been rigged.

I didn't see anything that looked troublesome.

I moved back to the cockpit, drew my pistol, and cautiously opened the hatch.

The boat didn't blow up.

I pushed into the salon with my weapon in the firing position and proceeded to clear the salon, the heads, the guest stateroom, and the master stateroom.

"Clear!" I shouted, holstering my pistol.

Archer climbed over the transom and I met her at the aft hatch in the salon. I decided it was a good idea to check the ignition lines and anything else that might trigger an explosive device.

I didn't find anything.

I had worked up a sweat putting in the new door, so I took a shower, then got dressed. "Do you want to go back to your place, or do you want to stay here?"

"Honestly, I'm torn. The plastic over my windows isn't going to stop anybody from coming in. I don't really want to leave the place unattended, but I also don't want to sleep in a place that lacks security."

"Let's stay here. If you want to get out of town, we can talk about taking the boat somewhere for a small vacation."

"Is this thing seaworthy?" she asked, half joking, half serious.

"It needs a little work. Okay, a lot of work. But, she hasn't sunk yet."

"I don't want to run from this problem. I want to get these bastards."

"You find any information about Votraxx Industries?"

"It's a holding company that's a subsidiary of another company. Which I'm sure is a subsidiary of something else, which will be equally as hard to track down. You know how these things work."

"I might be able to call in a favor and get some additional information."

Archer raised a curious eyebrow. "You know people with more intelligence assets than the FBI?"

"I do, actually," I said. "But every favor I call in costs me more than I want to pay."

Her eyes narrowed at me. "What's your real story?"

"No story," I said.

"Guy's like you just don't hang out on Coconut Key, volunteering as a deputy sheriff."

"I got tired of the rat race."

She surveyed me for a moment, probably making up all kinds of scenarios in her head about my past.

"No pressure. You can tell me as much, or as little, about yourself as you like. I mean, this isn't a real relationship. So I don't have those expectations."

I didn't say anything.

"So, what do we do? Sit back and wait for someone to attack again? One of these times they might be successful."

"They won't be successful," I said with confidence. "I can guarantee it."

She flashed me a skeptical glance. I had to admit, I was a little more concerned than I let on.

My phone rang, and Ashley's frantic voice filtered through the speaker. "Tyson, what the hell have you and JD gotten me into?"

"What's going on?"

"My house has been trashed. All of my computers have been taken. It looks like a fucking hurricane hit this place."

"Are you there now?"

"No. I'm not that stupid. I got out of there right away."

"Where are you?"

"Bumper."

"Stay put. I'm coming to get you. Don't go to the bathroom. Don't go outside. Make sure you are in plain view at all times. Nobody's going to do anything in front of an audience."

"Who did this?"

"I wish I knew."

"How much danger am I in?"

I wasn't going to sugarcoat it. "A lot."

She grumbled to herself. "You think a public place is going to stop a determined assassin?"

"Your odds are better in a public place. Hang tight. I'll be there as soon as I can."

"Hurry!"

30

I hoped we would get there in time.

We raced across town in an Uber and spilled out onto the curb in front of *Bumper*. The flash of my badge let us bypass the line, and we stormed inside without paying a cover.

Bumper was fairly crowded for a weekday evening. Techno music pumped through massive speakers, vibrating my chest. Of all the places Ashley could have picked, this was probably one of the worst.

Half of the crowd was chemically altered, dancing in a trance to the music. It was so loud, you could probably fire a gun and no one would notice. The club was dim and foggy, and multicolored lights slashed the air, swirling around the dance floor.

I scoured the tables by the main bar. I didn't see Ashley anywhere.

We made a lap around the club, searching for her. We checked the smokers' patio and the back hallway by the restrooms. I sent Archer into the ladies' room, and she returned a few moments later and shook her head.

There were three bars in the club, and I asked all the bartenders if they had seen a girl that matched Ashley's description. She was gorgeous and would stand out to any man with a heartbeat.

None of them had any recollection of her.

A text came through from Ashley's phone. *[Cooperate, or the girl dies.]*

I clenched my jaw. Mother fucker. They'd gotten to her first.

A tall, baldheaded man stepped up to us. He wore suit, dress shirt, no tie. The jacket could barely contain his broad shoulders and bulging biceps. If he wanted to, he could tear the back of the jacket just by flexing. He had a hand in his coat pocket, and I was relatively sure there was a pistol in there, aimed at me.

"Move," he said with a thick Russian accent. "Into the alley."

I exchanged a wary glance with Agent Archer. We turned around and strolled toward the back exit.

The baldheaded Russian mobster kept a safe distance from me.

We left the booming club behind as we pushed through the door and stepped into the alleyway. There were several other Russian mobsters waiting.

As soon as we had cleared the door, a strong hand grabbed

my arm and pushed me against the brick wall. The thugs frisked me and agent Archer. He found the pistol in my waistband and took it.

When he frisked Agent Archer, the goon made sure to get copious handfuls of her sumptuous assets.

"Watch it there, buddy!" she exclaimed.

He snickered, amused by her defiance.

That was the last thing I remembered. Someone cracked me in the back of the head with the grip of a pistol. Everything went black.

When I woke, the back of my head throbbed, and my knee and elbow were sore from hitting the pavement after I blacked out.

I don't know how long I was unconscious. I peeled open my eyes, taking in my surroundings. The gentle rocking told me I was on a boat. I lay on the deck with my hands tied behind my back with zip ties, and my ankles bound. My cheek rested against the cold decking.

I was in a small cabin. After a few attempts, I managed to stand and hop to the porthole. I was on the starboard side of the ship, and from this view, I couldn't see land. The running lights of the boat illuminated the small swells nearby. Beyond that was inky blackness.

A few minutes later, Baldy stormed into the compartment along with another man. His companion was a little shorter, and a little wider. Neither of them looked like they'd be fun to fight.

He grabbed me by the arm and dragged me out of the compartment. We were on a massive super-yacht. The thing must have been 160 feet long. It had three decks with a Jacuzzi on top. The main salon had a fully stocked bar, large screen TV, comfortable couches, and even a small pool table.

They brought me to the aft deck and sat me in a couch, not far from the swim platform.

The yacht was luxuriously appointed. The couch I sat on was made from supple Italian leather. Another goon stood at the transom, chumming the water. He dug out chunks of flesh from a slop bucket, filled with blood and meat.

I didn't like the looks of things.

Another man strolled out of the salon, holding a drink, with an unlit cigar in his hand. He wore a white T-shirt, white cargo shorts, and deck shoes. He looked like something out of a preppy catalogue, with the addition of a gold chain and several gold rings. He had a square jaw, steely blue eyes, and short blonde hair. I recognized him from *Forbidden Fruit*. Vladimir Kazakov.

The words came from his lips with a thick Russian accent. Can I get you something to drink?" Cigar, perhaps?"

"No, thank you."

"I'm leery of a man who turns down good liquor and fine Cuban cigars."

"I'm leery of a man who kidnaps people and takes them out to sea."

"Then we are leery of each other. As it should be."

My eyes flicked from him to the man chumming the water.

"Allow me to introduce myself. I am Vladimir Kazakov. I believe you have something that is of great importance to me."

"Looks like you already have everything. What could you possible want from me?"

"The data files the girl sent you."

"What data files?"

"Please don't insult my intelligence."

I figured there was no sense in bullshitting the man. "You've got my phone. You've got the data files."

"Those files contain some extremely incriminating information. If those fell into the hands of the authorities, it could bring down my entire empire. And that can't happen."

"Well, seeing how you have everything you need, how about you let us go, and we call it even?"

It was worth a try.

He laughed again. "I'm afraid that's not possible. See, data in this day and age is very difficult to control. You think it's safe, then the next thing you know, it's everywhere."

I shrugged. "The convenience of the modern age."

"I need to know if you've made copies? And if anyone else has access?"

"No copies. You've got Ashley's computer. You have my phone. That's it."

"What about your FBI friend? Does she have a copy? Has the data been disseminated to the Bureau?"

"No."

"What about your friend? The 80s has-been?"

"He can barely use email."

"I'd like to believe that. But I need to be sure. You see, I like my life here. I make a great deal of money, and as you can see, I live a life of luxury. But if the Feds have enough to put me away, I need to travel to greener pastures."

"I can assure you, you've acquired every copy of that data."

"I appreciate your cooperation. But I must be sure."

"Why'd you kill Kingston?" I asked.

"You should know the answer to that by now."

"I just want to hear it from you."

"I suppose there is no harm in telling you. It's not like you are going to live to tell anyone. He was stealing from me. And nobody steals from me."

Two more goons dragged Ashley through the salon, into the cockpit.

She'd been beaten. Her face was blue and black and purple. The sclera of her left eye was now red from a broken blood vessel. Her lip was split, and her hair was frazzled. She shivered and sobbed, and her face distorted with terror.

My body tensed and I struggled against the zip ties. I hated to see her like that. It was cruel and unnecessary.

Vladimir lit his cigar and puffed on it until the cherry glowed red. He exhaled a plume of smoke.

"I could torture you," Vladimir said to me. "But I think it would be far more effective if I tortured her and made you watch."

31

V ladimir took a heavy drag on his cigar, glowing the cherry red. I worried that he was going to burn Ashley with it, searing her flesh.

I had been captured and interrogated by enemy forces before. I knew I could withstand a high degree of pain, but I wasn't sure I could sit back and watch a young girl tortured for no reason.

Vladimir already had the truth. I had given him everything. There were no more copies of the data. There was nothing that could incriminate him, or his organization.

I struggled against my bonds, but I wasn't making any headway. It was possible to snap a zip tie if it was tight around your wrist. All you needed to do was slam it against your hip, and the cheap plastic would snap. But it didn't come without a price. It would hurt like hell, and the plastic would gouge your wrists. But it was a small price to pay for freedom.

Sitting on the couch with my hands behind my back, I

wasn't in the best position to attempt the maneuver. If I did snap it, Vladimir's goons would be on top of me in no time. And I still had the zip tie around my ankles to contend with.

Unfortunately, Vladimir had something much worse than cigar burns planned for Ashley.

Vladimir motioned for one of his goons to come over. The man held a pair of wire cutters. Two other goons held Ashley steady, while the third slipped the blades of the wire cutters around her pinky finger.

She bucked and convulsed and screamed, trying to free herself. But it was no use against men three times her size. Tears streamed from her cheeks, and the most horrible sound escaped her lungs.

"I'm going to ask you one more time. Are there any other copies?" Vladimir asked.

My face was red, and the veins in my neck bulged. My whole body tensed. Through gritted teeth I growled, "I told you. You have everything."

"You can't be too thorough in my line of work." He nodded to one of the goons. The man squeezed the wire cutters, and a loud snap filled the air as the jaws clamped tight, severing Ashley's pinky finger.

It's fell to the deck with a splat.

Red blood spurted from the stump. Ashley screamed bloody murder. Projectile tears launched from her eyes.

"Are you sure I have all the data?" Vladimir asked me again.

"You son-of-a-bitch!"

Vladimir chuckled. He nodded to his goons again.

The wire cutters clamped tight around Ashley's ring finger.

Snap!

Another finger hit the deck.

Another agonizing whale billowed from her lips.

"So, you are saying I have nothing to worry about?" Vladimir asked.

"You have everything," I shouted. "Let her go!"

Vladimir studied me for a moment. "I believe you. And I will let her go."

He nodded to his goons again, and they dragged Ashley toward the stern.

Vladimir flipped a switch, and lights underneath the water line illuminated the sea by the swim platform. Bull sharks swarmed the area like angry hornets. The water had been well chummed by now, and their appetites were insatiable.

My eyes widened with horror. I had seen a lot of despicable things in my life, but this ranked among the worst. "No. Don't do it, Vladimir!"

"You are all going to die one way or another. I find this way to be more entertaining."

Without hesitation, his goons pushed the gorgeous redhead into the water. Her screams were doused when she crashed into the sea. She flailed about on the surface kicking and screaming, which only made things worse.

To the sharks, Ashley looked like any other meal. They were

the vacuum cleaners of the sea, getting rid of the weak and wounded, the dead and dying. Flailing about on the surface was the worst thing you could do.

Within seconds, the hungry sharks attacked, turning the water red. The water splashed and sloshed as the hordes of sharks swarmed to take a chunk of flesh.

My stomach twisted, and a sour acidic taste of bile crept into the back of my throat. I'd seen my buddies on the battlefield hold in their guts with their hands. It was gruesome and grisly. But watching this young girl die in such a vicious way hit me like nothing I'd ever felt before. It was like someone had punched me in the gut, then pulled my heart out. I didn't know her well, but that didn't make it any less heart-breaking.

I was so mad, my eyes welled, my throat tightened, and I was sure I was frothing at the mouth. "I swear to God, I'm going to kill you."

As far as Vladimir was concerned, it was an empty threat. He knew I was the next one going into the water. "Get the FBI agent," he grumbled to a goon. Then he addressed me, "I'm going to ask you one last time. Is there another copy of those data files floating around on the Internet somewhere?"

I glared at him.

"Tell me the truth, and I will make it painless. I will put a bullet in your skull before I toss you in the water with those sharks."

32

I watched the sharks swirl around in the water as I stood at the edge of the swim platform. A goon had his meaty hand around my bicep, ready to shove me into the water.

I exchanged a concerned glance with Agent Archer who stood next to me, facing the same fate.

The remains of Ashley's body were unrecognizable, picked to the bone amid the white-capped frenzy of sharks.

We were next!

"Thank you so much for your cooperation," Vladimir said.

"Anytime," I replied with a healthy dose of sarcasm.

"Magnificent creatures, aren't they," Vladimir said. "Pure of purpose. Remorseless. Elegant."

"Deadly," I added.

"And fortunately the waters around Shark Cove are teeming with them."

He gave the nod, and his goons shoved us into the water.

I leapt off the platform, springing into the air as high as I could. I wanted to give myself an extra second of hang time. With my hands still restrained behind my back, I extended my arms as far as I could, then slammed them against my hips, snapping the zip-tie. The sharp plastic edges dug into my wrists. It hurt like hell, but at least my hands were free.

We plunged into the water, and Archer sank, unable to tread.

I saw gray and white and razor sharp teeth.

A shark bumped into me.

Then another.

It was an aggressive move. An exploratory action before the real attack. It was common for sharks to do a *bump and bite*. The outcome was not usually good for the intended target.

I saw another flash of fangs as a shark charged toward me. I punched the toothy bastard in the nose, sending it twisting away.

My heart pounded, and I could hear the thrashing sharks in the water. I reached into the pocket of my cargo shorts and pulled out my pocket knife.

Sharks swirled around me, not yet striking.

A few more bumps.

I extended the blade and cut through the zip-tie around my ankles. I clenched the knife between my teeth and swam to Archer. My hand grabbed her arm, and I pulled her deeper underwater.

Sharks typically feed around the surface. I pulled Archer underneath the boat, away from the swirling horde of flesh grinders. I cut her wrists and ankles free and continued swimming toward the bow.

My arms pulled me through the water, and my legs kicked frantically. My lungs burned, desperately needing oxygen. With my background, I was a much better swimmer than Archer, and I imagined that her lungs must have been on fire.

We had moved away from the frenzied pack. But a loan shark bumped Archer. It circled around, lowered its fin, then arched it spine. Its jaws opened and its serrated teeth sent chills down my spine.

It decided to sample Archer's leg.

Blood poured into the water as its teeth penetrated Archer's flesh.

I stabbed the monster in the eye with my knife.

The beast released its grip and spun around, swimming away, leaving a trail of blood.

Bubbles escaped from Archer's lips as she screamed underwater.

Her gaping puncture wound oozed blood, but fortunately the shark didn't take a fleshy chunk from her leg. He bit down, then released the moment I stabbed him in the eye.

We surfaced quietly near the bow, and I sucked in a huge breath of air. Archer fought back a scream.

Vladimir yelled at his goons, trying to figure out where we had disappeared to. He wasn't sure if we had been devoured.

I peeled off my T-shirt and cut it down the middle to add some length. Then I dove underwater, and tied it around the wound so Archer wouldn't bleed out.

I surfaced again. "Slow, steady breaths. Don't go into shock."

Archer's eyes were wide, and fear consumed her. The scent of blood was only going to attract more sharks. I kept a vigilant watch in the water, looking for predators.

The footsteps of goons stomping across the deck echoed through the night air. They looked over the gunwale, scanning the water.

We hugged the hull and moved forward to the anchor pocket. With the curve of the hull, it was difficult to see our position from above.

There were no lights in this position, and the sea looked like black ink. There was no telling how many sharks were out there, lurking in the darkness.

Archer needed immediate medical attention.

Vladimir and his goons scanned the water for signs of our demise.

The shark that I had stabbed in the eye drew the attention of his comrades. There was more blood and chaos in the water, and I think the other sharks attacked.

Vladimir assumed we had perished. After a few minutes, the massive chain rattled as the winch hoisted the anchor.

It didn't really matter whether the sharks got us. We were in the middle of the ocean. We were as good as dead. It was only a matter of time.

The ship's engines rumbled, and the yacht began to plow forward.

I took a deep breath, and Archer did the same. We dove underwater and pushed off the hull. I pulled myself through the inky blackness, swimming as far away from the yacht as possible. I stayed on pace with Archer who was doing her best despite the handicap.

I surfaced when she needed to come up for air. We took another breath, and plunged back under. By the second time we surfaced, we were far enough away not to be seen. The *Aquaholic* sailed away into the night, leaving a wake of white water in its path.

There were hundreds of sharks out there, Archer was bleeding, and we were alone in the water.

fter a few moments, my eyes adjusted to the darkness. Archer and I treaded water. I'd be lying if I said I wasn't concerned.

I scanned the horizon, trying to get my bearings. Vladimir had mentioned Shark Cove, which wasn't far from Starfish Key Island—*at least, by boat.*

It was a clear night, and the stars flickered in the heavens. You could see the hazy band that made the Milky Way— something that wasn't visible from the city. I glanced at the night sky, scanning the stars for orientation. Once I had figured out which direction north was, I looked for landmasses.

I didn't see any.

I knew Starfish Key had to be somewhere close by. Within a mile or two. Not an impossible swim, but not easy, especially under the circumstances.

Archer looked terrified. Her teeth chattered, and she shivered.

"We're going to be okay," I assured her.

"She didn't look too convinced.

"Starfish Key Island is not far in that direction," I said with confidence. I figured the more I believed we had a chance to succeed, the more she would too.

Archer was barely holding it together.

"We need to move at a steady pace and not attract attention. The more you look like a dying fish, the more appetizing you'll be."

Archer was dazed and numb.

We swam north. Thankfully, the water was relatively calm. But swimming at sea can be orders of magnitude more challenging than swimming in an Olympic size lap pool.

Fear and adrenaline made for good fuel. This was easy for me. My military background had prepared me well for long distance swims. The warm water off the Florida coast was nothing compared to the special ops I had pulled in frigid water where hypothermia could set in quickly.

It was tough on Archer.

She was a capable swimmer, but hadn't been trained for this kind of thing. Her arms turned to rubber quickly, and a few mouthfuls of saltwater made her feel like she was damn near drowning. The blood loss didn't help. She began to struggle around a thousand meters.

I paused for a moment, letting her catch her breath. There

was still no sign of land. For all I knew, we were swimming *away* from shore.

Archer's chest heaved for breath. She gasped, "I need to do more cardio at the gym."

It was good to see she still had a sense of humor, but Archer was losing blood, and getting weaker by the moment.

We floated up and down with the swells. As we crested the tip of a wave, I saw a small island maybe half a mile away. "Come on. We're almost there."

We continued our trek through the inky water. At 500 yards out, I saw Archer slip under the surface.

I dove under and pulled her up.

She coughed out a lungful of water, and I clung onto her and pulled her the rest of the way as she faded in and out of consciousness.

I dragged Archer to shore and rolled her onto her back.

"Archer! Archer!"

She peeled open her eyes and gazed at me.

Relieved she was still responsive, I said, "The tough part is over. We're going to get you help."

She nodded and reached a delicate hand to my face. A thin smile tugged at her lips, and in a weak, breathless voice she said, "You saved me."

I hadn't saved her yet. We were a long way from home, and she had lost a lot of blood.

Archer caught her breath in the wet sand as the surf nipped

at her ankles. She stared up at the stars. "I guess this is as good a place as any to die."

My face tensed, and I grew a lump in my throat. "You're not dying. That's a direct order."

"Aye-aye, sir." She gave a mock salute.

I climbed to my feet, my eyes surveying the island. Starfish Key was a small, desolate island with no permanent structures. In the day, you'd often find visitors anchored in the bay who'd taken a dinghy to the beach to enjoy the seclusion. Sometimes people would camp overnight, though it was prohibited.

I hoped to find some rule-breakers.

I moved to the tree line, and weaved through the tall grass and underbrush. There were mangrove trees, palms, a few cypress trees, and a host of other flora and fauna. In the distance I saw the faint flickering of firelight.

A spark of hope fluttered in my belly.

I raced back to the beach, scooped Archer in my arms, and hurried back into the underbrush. We crossed the small island in a few minutes. On the opposite shore, campers had built a fire.

We emerged from the foliage to see a man and woman roasting marshmallows, a dome tent pitched beside them on the beach.

My eyes quickly found their inflatable dinghy on shore. I saw a sailboat anchored in the bay, and breathed a sigh of relief.

Our presence startled them. They weren't expecting anyone to emerge from the forest—especially looking like we did.

The T-shirt around archers leg was now soaked with crimson blood. Her normally olive skin tone was now pale. She looked like the undead.

The woman was smoking a joint and gasped when she saw us. She was in her early 20s and had blonde curly hair that had been highlighted by the sun. She wore a pink bikini top and shorts.

The guy had dark hair and a narrow face and brown eyes. The girl was way out of his league. He wore a T-shirt and board shorts. It took his glassy eyes a moment to process what was happening.

"Call for help!" I shouted.

The guy dug into his pocket for a cell phone. "I can't get a signal."

"Shit," I grumbled to myself.

"Is that your boat?" I asked.

"Yeah," he nodded.

"Got a radio?"

He nodded again.

"Where are we?" I asked, As I moved toward the dinghy.

"Starfish Island."

"What happened?" the woman asked.

"Shark attack," I said.

The guy pushed the dinghy into the surf, and we climbed aboard. his girlfriend hopped in beside him, and he cranked up the electric motor.

"What's your name?" I asked as he spun us around and angled toward his sailboat. "I'm Garrett, and this is Becky."

The engine hummed as it drove us against the surf. Archer winced and groaned with pain as we crested the oncoming waves, the dinghy slapping back down against the surface, hard.

I held Archer's hand and told her everything was going to be okay, even though I was doubtful.

34

"Mayday, mayday, mayday!" Garrett shouted into the handset of the radio.

"Where's your first-aid?" I asked, frantic.

Garrett pointed at a storage compartment in the cabin. I pulled open the hatch and grabbed the supplies, then moved to Archer who lay on the lounge. I dug through the contents of the kit, looking for disinfectant and gauze.

"Mayday, mayday, mayday," Garrett repeated. "This is the *Zephyr*. We are just north of Starfish Key Island. There's been a shark attack. We need emergency medical assistance immediately!"

"*Zephyr*, this is Coast Guard Patrol 217. We are 3 miles north of your current position. We are in route now."

I took off the makeshift bandages. Now that I had proper supplies, I could secure the wound tightly and apply pressure to stem the bleeding.

Archer had puncture wounds in her calf in a c-shape. They

oozed blood, and flaps of flesh and muscle hung free. I could see the white bone underneath.

Archer screamed as I poured disinfectant over the wound, then wrapped gauze around her leg.

When the Coast Guard arrived, we transferred Archer to their patrol boat. I thanked Garrett and Becky as I boarded the medium-size response boat.

The engines roared, and the captain brought the boat on plane and we raced across the water to Coconut Key. Once I identified Archer as FBI, the Coast Guard contacted the Feds and the Sheriff's Department. An ambulance waited for us at the marina, and we were at Coconut Key General Hospital within a few minutes.

The EMTs pulled Archer out of the ambulance and wheeled her into the ER on a yellow gurney. A triage nurse assessed her wounds and took vital signs. Her heart rate, blood pressure, and oxygen saturation were all dangerously low. They gave her IV fluids, and once her vitals were stabilized, Archer was immediately taken to the OR.

"Do you think they'll be able to save her leg?" I asked the triage nurse.

"You'll have to speak with the doctor," she said with a grim look on her face.

Even if she had an opinion, she wasn't about to tell me. It wasn't her place. And she could probably lose her job if she said anything.

I took a seat in the waiting room amid sniffling children, people with broken bones, and old folks with oxygen tanks. It was freezing in the hospital, and my clothes were still damp. I felt like I was going to catch Ebola, or at least the flu, just sitting there.

A couple of kids sat at a children's table playing with blocks and puzzles. The pale green walls were depressing. TV news filtered through a flat screen mounted to the wall. Some talking head was blathering on.

I hoped to God that Archer came out of this okay. Though, I'm sure she wasn't going to be happy about the way her leg looked in heels anymore—if she still had the leg.

gents Miller and Hamilton stormed into the ER. They didn't see me at first, and made a beeline to the information desk. I overheard the receptionist inform them that Agent Archer was in surgery.

As I approached, Miller's disdainful eyes fell on me. "What happened?"

I told him everything, and Miller still looked at me like it was my fault. He clearly still had feelings for Archer. Not only was I the guy that took her away from him, I had damn near gotten her killed.

"The Coast Guard is looking for Vladimir, and I've got a tactical response team ready to go," I said.

"We'll handle this. I've contacted the Joint Interagency Task Force. We'll get that son-of-a-bitch." Miller handed me his card. "You call me the minute she's out of surgery."

"Will do."

"You should have called for backup at the first sign of trouble." His face flushed, and the veins around his temples bulged.

I said nothing.

Hamilton put a hand on Miller's shoulder, trying to diffuse his partner's anger. "Come on. Let's roll."

Miller glared at me for another moment, then the two stormed out of the ER.

I took a seat again and waited.

An hour later, the surgeon emerged, wearing sky-blue scrubs and a surgical mask pulled down around his neck. He had blue booties over his shoes, and a blue hair cover. "Mr. Wild?"

I stood up and rushed to greet him and nervously asked, "How did it go?"

"She's fine. She's resting in stable condition in a recovery area. You'll be able to see her shortly."

"Were you able to save the leg?"

"She had pretty extensive damage, but I was able to re-vascularize the leg. She'll need extensive physical therapy, but she should make a full recovery. She may have a little numbness and weakness in that leg which should resolve within 6 to 8 weeks, but it could take up to a year. The nurse will give you discharge instructions, along with prescriptions for pain medication, post surgical nausea, an anti-inflammatory, and a short course of antibiotics. I recommend she follow up in 14 days to remove the stitches."

"Great. Thank you."

He shook my hand and strolled back through the double doors into the patient area. After a few minutes, the nurse escorted me back to the recovery room.

IV fluids and antibiotics dripped into Archer's arm. Her heartbeat pulsed across a monitor which displayed blood pressure and oxygen saturation. All of her numbers were far better than when she was first admitted. Her groggy eyes found me as I took a seat beside her bed.

"How are you feeling?" I asked, as I took her hand.

"Like a fucking shark bit me," she slurred. "How do you think I feel?"

I chuckled. "Doc says your going to be okay."

"I'm certainly not going to be okay. My miniskirt days are over."

"I'm sure you will look just fine in a miniskirt."

"I think it's going to be long pants for me from here on out." Her eyes brimmed. "But, at least I still have it."

I agreed.

A nurse stroked the bottom of her foot, checking her sensation. "Can you wiggle your toes for me?"

Archer winced as she tried to move them, but the little piggies weren't keen on going to market. They moved about a millimeter, which was better than not moving at all.

"That's good," the nurse said.

It would be a long time before Archer was duty ready again, if ever. And by the look on her face, that realization was sinking in.

"From what I know of you, you'll bounce back from this," I said.

"I appreciate the confidence."

"In the meantime, you can binge a bunch of Netflix shows. Catch up on your reading."

"Do you know when they're discharging me?"

"I don't. I would imagine they'd want to keep you overnight, but with the way insurance is these days, they might kick you out this afternoon."

"I might need a little assistance around the house. Think you might be up for it?"

"Sure," I said in a comforting tone. "Whatever you need."

"Whatever? That's pretty open-ended. There's a lot of stuff that needs to be done around the house."

"I'll see what I can do about getting those windows replaced. You might want to consider staying somewhere else until the house is secure."

"What about Vladimir?"

"Miller's working on that now. With any luck, they'll have him in custody soon. Don't worry about him. He's going down. No question about it."

36

They released Archer the next day. A nurse pushed her out of the hospital in a wheelchair, and I helped her into a cab and took her home. I had a pocket full of discharge instructions, a pair of crutches, and a handful of prescriptions that I had filled at the pharmacy attached to the hospital.

I got Archer situated in bed, brought her a glass of water and some pudding, dosed her up on her pain meds, and let her sleep.

I let agent Miller know that Jen was safe and resting at home. He said they had located Vladimir, and were planning to take him down. He didn't want my assistance. I asked him to inform me when they had Vladimir in custody. A few hours later, I saw on the 10 o'clock news that the FBI in a coordinated effort with the Coast Guard had arrested Vladimir.

The footage on the news showed Vladimir being escorted in handcuffs into the county jail.

The news cut to an interview with Vladimir's attorney. "My client is innocent of the charges. He has done no wrong. And I look forward to clearing my client's name. He is an upstanding member of the community, a benefactor in several local charities, and has no criminal record."

I was thrilled to see the scumbag arrested, and mildly perturbed that Miller hadn't informed me.

I called Sheriff Daniels. "What do you know?"

"I know that he's in Federal custody," Daniels said. "Beyond that, they aren't sharing much information. When he kidnapped a federal agent, this became a federal matter. I asked that they keep me in the loop. But I'm not keeping my fingers crossed." He sighed. "How is your FBI friend doing?"

"She's okay. It's going to be a long recovery."

"You think Vladimir killed Kingston?"

"I can all but prove it."

"Well, it looks like he's going to go down for a long time. So, we might not get him on Kingston, but it's not like he's going to walk away." I appreciate the work you guys did."

"Sure thing." I asked him to keep me updated, then I called JD to see how things were going with Scarlett.

JD was still in Miami. "I think I'm going to stay here for a few days just to keep an eye on things. I want to be close by in case something happens."

"Like what?"

"Like that little devil escaping. I'm sure if there is a way out of that facility, Scarlett will find it."

I caught JD up to speed on everything that had happened.

"I go out of town for 24 hours and all hell breaks loose."

I chuckled.

"I'm sorry about your girlfriend."

"She's not my girlfriend."

"You have serious commitment issues."

"You're one to talk," I said. "How's Belinda?"

JD let out a depressed side. "She went back to Mississippi, or wherever she was from."

"I'm sure you'll find a replacement in no time."

"Damn skippy."

"Send Scarlett my best," I said.

"Will do."

I hung up, grabbed a beer from the fridge, and sat on the couch, watching the rest of the news. I ended up crashing there so I wouldn't disturb Archer as she slept.

I woke up in the morning to the smell of bacon and coffee. My face twisted with confusion.

I wiped the sleep from my eyes to see Archer crutching around in the kitchen, fixing breakfast. I pulled myself off the couch. "What are you doing?"

"I owe you a breakfast. It's the least I can do. After all, you did save my life."

I frowned at her. "Get back in bed. I'll make breakfast. You don't need to be up. You need to keep that foot elevated and let the swelling go down."

"I am not going to start acting like an invalid."

"At least give yourself a chance to heal. Plus, you're on some pretty heavy duty pain meds."

"It's just breakfast. It's not heavy machinery."

"Just try to take it easy."

"Yes, Daddy," she said in a girly voice.

I took over breakfast and made her get back into bed. I pampered her for the rest of the day.

Not long after breakfast, an insurance adjuster stopped by to look at the front door, the windows, and the damage to the siding from the car explosion. He didn't say much, and noted everything in a laptop computer. Said the insurance company would be in touch.

JD gave me the number of a guy who was great with replacement windows. He came out the next day and gave an estimate. The house was older, and the windows weren't very energy efficient. Archer would have to wait to see what the insurance settlement would be before making a decision on doing the whole house.

The next few days were up and down. Jen was progressing well, but dealing with bouts of depression over the injury. Covered up by bandages, she had no idea what her leg looked like, and she was envisioning the worst.

It was about a week later when the really bad news came.

37

"**Y**ou have got to be shitting me," Archer shouted into the phone.

Rage boiled on her astonished face. She was talking to her boss, Special Agent Dalton.

"That is total bullshit!" Archer griped.

I mouthed the word, *"What?"*

My curiosity had been piqued. But I knew this wasn't good news.

"I know. I know," Archer replied into the phone, trying to calm herself down. She took a deep breath. "Okay. Thanks for letting me know."

She hung up.

Her eyes filled with exasperation. "You are not going to believe this."

"I'm listening."

"The judge tossed the case."

"What?"

"Miller raided Vladimir's boat before the judge had signed off on the search warrant."

I grumbled.

"That's not the worst of it. The Office of Professional Responsibility has been investigating him for months. It turns out there are 14 complaints against Miller. Falsifying evidence. Compelling perjury. Taking bribes. The list goes on. There is evidence he tipped off several traffickers about law enforcement efforts. I think he may have been our inside leak. The judge said, 'Mr. Miller's conduct taints this investigation to a level that brings into question the credibility of the entire agency and everyone involved.'"

Anger welled within me, but I remained calm.

"I knew there was a reason I never liked that guy," Archer grumbled.

I knew exactly what I had to do. In that moment, I began formulating a plan. I had watched Vladimir kill an innocent girl, and I wasn't going to let him get away with it. He had caused Archer irreparable harm. My whole policy of letting the system take care of things went out the window. It wasn't that I believed the system was broken, but there were way too many cracks and holes.

"Just relax." I said, trying to calm Archer down. "A guy like Vladimir will get what's coming to him."

Archer's eyes brimmed. "It's not fair. These creeps always get away with it. They get the best lawyers, they bribe judges, they pay off jurors..."

She broke down, sobbing. Her chest heaved with jerks, and rivers of tears streamed down her cheeks.

I crawled in bed beside her, slung my arm around her shoulder, and tried to comfort her. Archer was at an emotional breaking point, and Vladimir walking away scot-free was the last straw.

"Don't worry. You'll be back on the street in no time, putting away bad guys."

She wiped her eyes and sniffled. "Look at me. I'm a mess. You must think I'm so weak?"

"I think you're very brave. You've been through a lot. Why don't you cut yourself some slack?"

She hugged me tight.

"You win some, you lose some. But you live to fight another day. There will be other opportunities, I assure you."

She wiped her eyes. "I promise, this is the last time I cry."

"Doubtful, but if you say so."

She smacked my chest playfully. "I'm really not a crier, though it would appear otherwise."

"We need to get you out of the house. Have a little fun in the sun. You've been cooped up in here for a week. That's enough to make anybody go mental. How about we go for a ride in the boat?"

"Um, No. I don't want to go anywhere near the water."

"You know what they say about falling off the horse."

"Yeah, well, horses don't have razor-sharp teeth."

I raised my hands in surrender. "Okay. Fine. We'll get back out on the water on your timetable. How about we go to *Tsunami Jack's* for lunch? Grab a few daiquiris. But not too many," I cautioned, her margarita experience coming to mind.

"Shut up."

"Then maybe you can operate some heavy machinery—if you think you're healthy enough for sexual activity."

She gave me a look.

"If you're not up to it, I totally understand."

It had been a week since we bumped uglies, and I was feeling a little overstocked. My troops were begging to be deployed.

"I can assure you. I'm more than healthy enough."

She leaned in and kissed me with her full lips. "Thank you, for taking care of me," she whispered in my ear. "I know this wasn't in our original contract. I promise, I will give you bonus compensation."

"Sounds good to me."

One thing led to another, and we didn't make it to *Tsunami Jack's* for lunch. It was happy hour by the time we got there. And Archer was definitely healthy enough. Though, we did have to approach the situation delicately.

That evening, I called JD and caught him up to speed. "You up for something a little crazy?"

38

I swore this was something I was never going to do again. But here I was. Ready to do it. Sure, I made all kinds of justifications in my mind. *It was an extenuating circumstance*, I told myself. *He deserved it*, I said. I was *righting a wrong*.

It was all bullshit.

I wanted to kill the man, plain and simple.

He was a scumbag.

Still, in the back of my mind, I knew that this was exactly the kind of thing that had purchased me a one-way ticket to hell. I was supposed to be redeeming myself. But I was digging a deeper hole.

Fuck it!

In that moment, I didn't care.

I was angry.

If I was going to hell for serving up justice, so be it. The Big

Man upstairs wasn't doing anything about it. The world was full of atrocities. Injustice. Evildoers. Despicable people. And many of them went through life without suffering any repercussions.

Where is the fairness in that?

Going to hell would be a small price to pay to get a guy like Vladimir Kazakov off the streets.

I had waited patiently for the opportune moment to arrive.

It was here.

Vladimir's yacht was docked at the Coconut Key Yacht Club, resupplying. Crew personnel shuffled back and forth, carrying food, water, and supplies. It was after midnight, and goons stood on the dock with machine guns. I recognized the baldheaded thug that I'd encountered at *Bumper*.

I grabbed a box from the back of the supply truck, hefted it on my shoulder, and walked down the dock amid the rest of the crew personnel. I wore a baseball cap, and made sure to keep the box blocking my face as I passed the machine gun wielding goons. I stepped aboard at the stern, walked down the passageway along the port side, then spiraled down the stairway to the crew quarters and stowage areas.

I set the box down, then spun around and marched back up the steps to the passageway. Instead of heading aft, I moved forward.

I peered through a window, into the salon—it was empty.

I continued forward and climbed a staircase to the second deck. Flattening my back against the bulkhead, I peered into the upper deck salon. Vladimir enjoyed a drink with a luscious blonde who was clearly only there because of money.

I slid my pistol from its holster and screwed on a suppressor to the end of the barrel.

Ice rattled in Vladimir's glass as he finished his drink. He handed the empty glass to his companion. "Fix me another, would you?"

She took his glass and stood up from the sofa and sauntered her high heels across the deck to the bar. Vladimir's eyes followed her pert assets. She had a sway that was hypnotic.

She reached the bar and scrunched up her face and pouted. She whined, "Baby, we're out."

"Be a doll and go downstairs. There's another bottle in the main bar."

"Sure thing, babe."

I ducked away from the portal and flattened my back against the bulkhead as she sauntered in my direction. I was on the forward side of the hatch. She stepped into the passageway, and turned aft without seeing me.

I exhaled a relieved breath.

It was my opportunity to strike.

I waited until she descended the steps, then I rounded the corner and stormed the salon. My weapon was in the firing position, and I took aim at Vladimir.

He sat on the couch, fiddling with his phone. He didn't see me for the first few steps. When he looked up, his eyes rounded with horror.

I wanted him to see who the angel of death was. But that was my undoing. In the moment I hesitated, one of his goons had stepped into the salon.

The bang of gunfire filled my ears, and bullets snapped in my direction.

Glass shattered, and wood splintered as the bullets pelted the cabinetry and mirror behind the bar.

I hit the deck and scampered behind a couch as a torrent of bullets screamed at me.

Vladimir sprang to his feet and scurried out of the salon. He dashed into the master stateroom and sealed the hatch behind him.

I popped up, aiming my weapon over the couch. My finger squeezed the trigger, sending 9mm slugs across the salon. The bullets hammered into the goon, spraying a geyser of blood from his chest. He fell back against the bulkhead and slid to the floor, blood pooling around his body.

More of Vladimir's thugs were on their way. I heard them shouting to each other on the deck below, their heavy footsteps trampling closer.

This was a bad position to be in. I was about to get flanked.

39

I dashed across the salon into the starboard side passageway.

Two goons raced up the steps, and blasted a few rounds at me. Bullets snapped through the air, inches from my skin. The goons managed to get off a few haphazard shots, but they didn't hit shit. It takes a trained professional to hit a moving target while on the run—these guys were street criminals.

I returned fire.

Blood erupted as I peppered them with bullets. Their bodies crashed to the stairs.

Most gun battles occur within a few feet, and 90% of the shots miss. I may have been outnumbered, but I was playing with a considerably better kill ratio.

Another goon rounded the corner and entered through the port-side hatch.

I spun around and squeezed off two more rounds that

crossed the salon. The bullets nicked him in the arm, and the impact spun him around. He had an uzi machine-gun and he sprayed a hailstorm of bullets as his finger clenched the trigger.

I ducked behind the bulkhead for cover as the projectiles tore through the fiberglass hull.

I spun around and fired two more shots, tapping the goon in the chest. He staggered back to the hatch, then tumbled over the gunwale.

I heard a splash into the water below.

The yacht's standard crew took cover, sheltering below deck. The ones on the dock, loading supplies, took off running. They were just hired hands, and weren't about to get into this fight.

Another goon charged up the starboard stairs. Muzzle flash flickered as he sprayed bullets at me.

I ducked back into the salon and crouched down behind the couch where Vladimir had been sitting. I looked through the windows of the salon.

I couldn't see the goon, and I assumed he was down low, crawling against the deck toward the hatch of the salon.

I inched aft toward the sky lounge, moving around the end of the couch. I hovered below the arm rest.

Behind me, the sky lounge contained another sofa, two chairs, and a coffee table. It was open-air, and would have been too vulnerable a position. I'd be an easy target from the upper sundeck.

The goon slung his weapon through the starboard hatch

and opened fire. Bullets strafed the top of the couch, sending stuffing floating into the air.

I flattened myself against the deck, then angled the barrel of my pistol around the back of the couch and opened fire.

I caught the goon in his kneecap.

The joint exploded, sending a mix of bone and blood splattering against the bulkhead.

He screamed in agony as he dropped to his good knee.

Another quick shot put a bullet through his head.

He flopped to the deck, chunks of his skull and brain oozing down the bulkhead behind him.

Another thug angled his weapon around the port-side hatch and sent another flurry of bullets at me.

I crawled around the back of the couch as bullets plowed through the cushion. They exited the back of the couch, missing me by inches as I flattened against the deck.

I glanced at the glass windows on the starboard side. In the reflection, I could see the goon as he darted behind the bar.

I grabbed a piece of debris and heaved it across the salon, clattering against the deck by the starboard hatch.

The goon popped up like a prairie dog, angling his weapon over the top of the bar, firing in the direction of the noise.

I sprang into action and squeezed off two more rounds, sending him crashing back against the liquor bottles. The glass shelving broke, and the bottles crashed down, smashing against the deck.

I pressed the mag release button, dropped the magazine out, and slapped another one in. I pulled the slide back, charging a round, then sprang to my feet.

I had my eye on the hatch to the master stateroom. My target was beyond that door.

But just as I took a step, I heard another goon behind me. He had jumped down from the sundeck and landed in the sky lounge.

I spun around and fired before he could get a shot off. He tumbled back and smashed the glass coffee table, sending shards of glass clattering across the deck. It was the bald guy from the club.

I couldn't be sure, but I think he was the last of Vladimir's goons.

I turn around and stormed toward the master stateroom. Glass and debris crunched underneath my feet. I knew Vladimir would be waiting on the other side with some heavy artillery.

But I had something special in mind for him.

I stood aside and fired a couple rounds into the locking mechanism.

Just as I had anticipated, Vladimir was waiting on the other side, locked and loaded.

Kaboom!

The thunderous roar of a shotgun blasted, shredding the hatch and knocking it from the hinges.

Vladimir had done my work for me.

In his case, he had fired too soon. Gun smoke filled the compartment, and the sharp smell of gunpowder wafted to my nostrils. I pulled a fragmentation grenade from my cargo pocket. I tossed it into the stateroom, then dove for cover behind the couch.

An instant later the grenade detonated, spraying blistering bits of shrapnel in all directions. Bulkheads rumbled, and the deck quaked.

Vladimir's screams filled the air.

The deafening blast left me with a high pitch ringing in my ears. A milky haze filled the compartment.

I climbed to my feet and advanced toward the stateroom, cautiously. When I peered in, I saw Vladimir's mutilated body on the deck.

He was still alive, and blood gurgled in his lungs.

I stepped into the compartment and hovered over him. His eyes fixed on me as his body twitched and convulsed. He could barely choke out a few words with his esophagus filled with blood. He managed to say, "See you in hell," before dying.

He was probably right.

40

I darted out of the master stateroom, raced through the salon, and headed forward in the outer passageway. The crew were all sheltering below deck. There was no one in the area.

I dove off the bow into the water below and pulled myself down to the bottom where I had stashed the Dräger, a pair of fins, and a mask.

It was a military issue Dräger LAR V closed-circuit oxygen rebreather that Jack had acquired from his *source*. It was the preferred diving apparatus for stealth units. Low noise, no bubbles, compact and streamlined. The perfect way to move in and out of a harbor undetected.

The water was near black, but a small waterproof tactical flashlight helped me find my rig. I donned the gear, cleared the mask, and swam out of the marina, heading for the open ocean.

JD waited for me in the *Slick'n Salty* about a mile offshore. I climbed onto the swim platform, and scaled the transom. JD helped with my gear. "How'd it go?"

"How did what go?" I replied with a grin.

"Good answer."

He tossed me a towel, and I dried off. I peeled out of my clothes, and changed into a fresh set. I stuffed a few rocks in the pocket of my cargo shorts, and stuffed the shirt inside and tossed them into the water. There were traces of gunpowder and blood spatter on my clothing. It had most likely been washed away during my swim, but why take a chance?

It was never a good idea to keep a weapon around that had been involved in a crime, so I dismantled the pistol and sent it to Davy Jones locker as well.

JD had a fishing line in the water. He had pulled almost a dozen yellowtail snapper out of the sea while he was waiting. I took it over and reeled in the line as he climbed to the bridge and cranked up the engines.

It was a clear night, the stars flickered overhead.

Once the line was clear, JD brought the boat on plane and we moved to another reef a few miles away and fished some more.

Jack grabbed a few beers from the galley, and we cast our lines and acted like nothing had happened.

It wasn't long before I got a call from Sheriff Daniels. "Thought you might like to know Vladimir Kazakov isn't breathing anymore."

"What happened?" I asked, innocently.

"Somebody took him out. It's a bloodbath. Professional job."

"Couldn't have happened to a nicer guy."

"I couldn't agree more. Feds are crawling around the scene now."

"Any leads?"

"The security camera footage from the marina wasn't very useful. There was birdshit on the lens. The crew is saying it was a team of guys. They don't know how the hit squad accessed the boat. They were like phantoms, the crew said. I'm guessing a rival organization?"

"Could be," I said.

"Anyway, I thought you'd like to know."

"Thanks for the heads up. Do you need us for anything?"

"No. There's already too many running around this crime scene." Daniels paused. "Where are you right now?"

My heart stammered slightly. "Fishing snapper with Jack."

"Catching anything?"

"Mostly yellowtail."

"Save some for me."

"You got it." I hung up the phone.

"Think he knows?" Jack asked.

"He suspects," I said. "I think he just wanted to call and find out where we were and make sure we had an alibi."

"It's a weak one," JD said.

"Trust me, nobody's gonna look too hard into this," I said, hopeful.

We took smiling selfies with large yellowtail dangling from hooks. It would a least prove we were out on the water, and the geo-tags would confirm our location.

The next day, the news reported that Vladimir had been killed by a rival syndicate. And that was the last I heard about the incident.

Archer knew better than to ask questions, but I think she suspected. She was relieved to hear of Vladimir's demise, but the incident had left her scarred—and not just physically.

Her recovery was progressing well, and she was regaining strength in the leg, though there was still some residual numbness. She had been working hard with physical therapy, but she was mostly behind a desk now. And that was driving her crazy.

She wasn't sleeping well, and would frequently wake up in the middle of the night screaming, in a cold sweat. She didn't like to talk about the event, and kept it all in. The stress of it all seemed to make her more emotional, and she broke down frequently.

I could relate to what she was going through. Anybody who'd ever been in a life and death situation had to deal with the aftermath at some point. She was seeing a therapist, and going to support groups.

I tried to be there for her as much as I could.

Our *Friends with Benefits* was progressing into something

more, even though neither of us spoke about it. So, I was a little surprised when she told me she might be leaving Coconut Key.

41

The day I was dreading finally came. There was a handshake, and funds were exchanged.

Jack sold the boat.

And I was homeless.

"It's just temporary," Jack assured me as we stood on the dock, watching the new owner take the boat out of the marina. "I just need some available cash while I'm going through this thing with Scarlett. That lawyer knows how to do one thing really well—bill."

"I've got cash if you need it." I had all of my personal belongings stowed in a large duffel bag.

Jack had taken all the diving gear and equipment earlier. "Well, to tell you the truth. I've had my eye on something a little... bigger."

"Another boat?"

"A 65 footer. I just don't want to take the plunge until I get through this little patch."

"How's Scarlett doing?"

"She's okay. Back at home. On the straight and narrow. She gets up, goes to work, comes home. I'm trying to stay on top of the situation. She's got a court date coming up next month, and hopefully, we can get the whole thing dismissed. You're more than welcome to crash on the couch until I get another boat."

"Jen said I could stay with her."

"When's the wedding?" Jack jabbed.

"Oh, no! No wedding. We are just doing the casual thing."

"That's how it always starts," JD said with a grin.

"I don't know. She's thinking about leaving the bureau and Coconut Key."

Jack's jaw dropped. "Really?"

"That whole incident is really fucking with her head."

Jack frowned. "I'm sorry to hear that."

We strolled down the dock to the parking lot when my phone rang. It was Isabella. I had spoken to her shortly after the demise of Vladimir. She was pleased that Archer believed the internal leak was Agent Miller, and her investigation of Muerte Dolorosa was on the back burner. I wasn't sure what she wanted now.

"Just thought I'd give you a heads up. I located Cartwright. Just thought you'd like first crack at him. After all, he did screw you over in Mexico."

I hesitated for a moment. Did I even want to know? Did it matter anymore?

"You're not going to let him get away with that, are you?"

After a long moment, I said, "Send somebody else. I'm totally Zen about it now."

"You don't want everyone to think you've gone soft, do you?"

"Where's he at?" I couldn't help but ask.

"Right now, he's in Monaco. I'll give you till the end of the day to make up your mind. One way or another, he needs to be dealt with. I can't have agents going rogue. It looks bad on the Corporation."

I tried desperately to maintain my state of detachment. But the more I thought about it, the more it gnawed at me. The man had put a bullet in my chest, and I had almost died.

I *did* die, for a moment or two.

But, maybe it was his bullet that saved me? His bullet that changed my life and gave me a second chance to change my fate?

I sure as hell was screwing my second chance up.

"I'll think about it," I said and hung up.

I tucked my duffel bag into the backseat of Jack's Porsche and climbed into the passenger seat.

JD threw the car into gear, let out the clutch, and the fat tires spewed gravel as we peeled out of the parking lot. He whisked me to Archer's house. As we pulled into the drive-way, I got a text from Aria.

"Hey, got a shoot in Monaco next week. Why don't you meet me there? Some rich oil sheik is loaning me his yacht for the week. We'll have a blast?"

I took a deep breath as I tried to decide how to respond. I showed JD the message.

"I'm not touching that with a 10 foot pole. That's all you, pal."

It was an odd coincidence. Was the universe trying to tell me something?

Ready for more?
The adventure continues with Wild Riviera!

Join my newsletter and find out what happens next.

AUTHOR'S NOTE

Wow! Thank you! The response to the first book has been so great. Thanks to everyone who left a great review. I'm having a blast writing Tyson's adventures, and I hope you continue to enjoy them.

Thanks for reading!

—*Tripp*

TYSON WILD

MAX MARS

The Orion Conspiracy

Blade of Vengeance

The Zero Code

Edge of the Abyss

Siege on Star Cruise 239

Phantom Corps

The Auriga Incident

Devastator

CONNECT WITH ME

I'm just a geek who loves to write. Follow me on Facebook.

www.trippellis.com

Made in the USA
Las Vegas, NV
05 November 2021